The Author is a 48-year-old sports journalist, who loves to read and write, taking a first step to being a published writer.

His other interests include films, travel, food and playing and watching sports.

Roddy lives alone in the picturesque East Yorkshire village of Howden.

To find out more about the author visit:

www.roddybrooks.com

THE JOURNEY

I would like to dedicate this book to my parents, Peter and Rose Brooks. They will forever be in my heart.

Roddy Brooks

THE JOURNEY

AUSTIN MACAULEY
PUBLISHERS LTD.

A CIP catalogue record for this title is available from the British Library.

Illustrations by Michael Ezaky

ISBN 978 184963 392 5

www.austinmacauley.com

First Published (2014)
Austin Macauley Publishers Ltd.
25 Canada Square
Canary Wharf
London
E14 5LB

Printed and bound in Great Britain

Acknowledgments

I would like to acknowledge the following for their help:

Natalie Bowen; Kirstie Lovewell; Gemma Roberts; Rory Dollard; Terry Elston.
With special thanks to Olivia Bunn.

THE JOURNEY

Part one of *the Land of the Hiding* Tree trilogy

Chapter 1

Livi threw open the curtains and cast her gaze across the deep valley of Ethmyra. She was a princess but she didn't feel that made her special. She felt special because she was lucky to live in such a wonderful place with such wonderful friends. The little princess also knew she was special for one other reason. She could make people love one another just by willing it. If she wanted to make something happen – as long as it was a nice thing – she could make it happen. Wherever she went and whatever she said people just became instantly happy. Even bad things became good when she sang her beautiful songs. But not everything in the land of Ethmyra was happy or peaceful, or as Livi would like it. Some time ago her father, the king, had to go away to fight demons. Now he spent a lot of time in a different land and that made Livi sad because the king and Queen Deborah, her mother, could not be together. Although she had come to accept this she was sad because of it, even though she did want everyone to be happy. And now even her brother Prince Nathaniel, who sometimes teased her and could be a real pig, had also gone away. He had gone off on a crusade and she missed him and loved him.

"Why should Nathan be having all the fun?" she asked herself.

Just then she heard a noise, an animal noise off in the distance. Livi strained to hear what had made the noise and when she recognised it a broad smile spread across her face. It was a dog, but not just any dog. It was her dog, Dillon, the faithful hound who kept guard at the foot of her bed every night, keeping her safe as she dreamt the night away.

"Dillon, Dillon, it's lovely to see you," shouted Livi from the balcony.

With that she turned tail and ran out of her bedroom and down the staircase to greet her dog. Just as Dillon bounded up to the front steps Livi burst through the great oak doors of the palace and they collided in a sea of hugs and kisses and licks.

"Oh I love you Dillon, so much," said a delighted Livi.

"I love you too, my princess," said Dillon.

Yes, in case you were wondering, Dillon could talk. It was one of the many magical things in the magical kingdom of Ethmyra.

"Alas, I bring bad tidings I am afraid my princess," added the dog between breaths as he fought to bring his racing heart under control. For not only had he been racing at great speed from far away but he was also very excited to see his mistress.

"Why, what ails you?" enquired Livi.

Dillon proceeded to tell the princess of trouble that had entered the land of Ethmyra. On the far reaches of what was mostly a peaceful land there was a realm ruled with malice and spite by a witch known as Lady Half-Trousers. Livi often thought that was a strange name but it had been explained to her by Yksboor, the brave knight who dedicated his life to keeping evil at bay in the kingdom. She was called Lady Half-Trousers because she thought she was a lady, although few agreed, and also because her trousers only came halfway down her legs, or half-mast as a sailor might say.

As if a witch was not trouble enough, that part of the land also had a dragon called Tremgara who delighted in attacking villages, killing the animals and stealing all of the treasure that people had worked hard to save. Tremgara also had a daughter, Raygon, who like her mother liked to terrorise the villagers.

Livi was not afraid of the witch or the dragons as she knew she could protect herself, that's what magic powers were for. And she also knew the people would be safe as long as Yksboor was there to defend them. Queen Deborah had told her that. For although she was old, and she was very old or so it seemed to Livi, she was also very, very wise. She was almost always right but Livi wasn't brave enough or clever enough to think she could get away with arguing about the fact. Not for many years yet, anyway.

But what Dillon had to tell Livi chilled her to the bone and she shuddered at the thought of what he had to say. Yksboor had lost a long and bloody battle with the two dragons and the rest of the forces of evil. He was locked away in a foul-smelling dungeon in a castle in the land ruled by Lady Half-Trousers.

"Oh what could be done?" Livi thought to herself. She would ask her mother for she would know what to do. And then she remembered her mummy had gone to a far-off realm of the kingdom to converse matters of state with her own mother. So there was no other answer. The princess would have to rescue Yksboor herself. And Dillon would have to help her do it.

"Come Dillon, we must rescue the knight so he can keep the kingdom safe until my mummy returns," she said.

"But is that wise?" enquired the dog who was well known among the animals for being a very wise dog who often thought long before doing anything. Some people thought he sometimes thought too long before taking action but he didn't really care about that. As long as he spent long enough thinking things through he knew the right answer would come to him eventually. Dillon's best thinking was always done when he was asleep so he curled up on the floor and closed his eyes.

"Don't go to sleep on me – that's so like you Dillon. I don't believe it," said the princess.

"What's wrong?" asked the dog.

"We need to go and we need to go now," replied Livi.

"OK, I'm coming," said Dillon, shaking his head and muttering to himself under his breath.

"I heard that and, what's more, I know what it meant," said Livi as she fixed the dog with a steely glare.

Chapter 2

Finding The Hiding Tree was never a problem. It was off Hiding Tree Lane, which was off The Hiding Tree Highway. Everyone knew where it was. Gaining entry to The Hiding Tree was another question entirely. Anyone with darkness in their hearts could not go inside and be accepted into the sanctuary which protected against all things evil.

On many occasions frightened travellers had faced the gut-wrenching choice of being parted from one of their party because The Hiding Tree just refused to open its welcoming entrance and grant them shelter. And more often than not those refused entry didn't even realise, or refused to accept, that they carried the darkness in their heart which barred them from entering into its cavernous safety.

Nobody knew how The Hiding Tree got there or how it came about. Surely something so good could not be a simple tree, its power must be drawn from something magical. Yet nobody ever came up with a convincing reason for its existence.

Most people, like Livi, just knew of it. It wasn't like she had been told about it, it was just like a memory so powerful that the first time she needed it the desire for sanctuary placed a picture of it in her mind. That picture also became a map of how to get there. Livi remembered the day clearly when her mother had tried to tell her about it, stopping her mid-sentence with the terse line: "I already know of it, Mummy!" When asked how she knew she just shrugged her shoulders and said she didn't know why but just that she knew about it anyway.

Anyway there was no time for that now. Once Livi and Dillon had been granted access to The Hiding Tree it was as if they had been transported to a different land. A wide hallway led to winding stairs which seemed to go ever downward.

Walking down the steps it felt as if they were being swallowed by the earth. There was no need to wonder which way to go as the knowledge was magically transferred into the mind of anyone who sought, and was granted, shelter in The Hiding Tree. Although the steps seemed never-ending there was no burden on the mind. It was as if all cares were removed just by being in this safest of places. And there was no need to check your steps as the ever-burning light illuminated the way. Livi called it smelly fire because the methane gas used to fuel the lights did have a bit of a pong. That, however, was of little consequence because smelly and safe was preferable to fragrant but in fear. The companions had sought out The Hiding Tree, not because they were in imminent danger but because they knew it was a safe place to rest and gather their thoughts for the long and perilous journey that lay ahead.

Livi and Dillon talked long into the evening until the princess eventually fell asleep against the dog, a protective paw placed across her shoulder.

When she awoke Livi knew exactly what she must do. It was as if she had been told. As she had slept she dreamed deeply and heard her mother's voice as if she was talking clearly to hear. "Seek out the Sisters of Solace," her mother had said in the dream.

"Ah, good, you are awake. Did you sleep well my princess?" asked Dillon.

"Yes, thank you," replied Livi as she wiped the tiredness from her blinking eyes.

"And what did the Queen tell you to do?" asked Dillon.

The question came to him automatically. He had awoken during the night and heard Livi talking to her mummy as she slept.

"She said we must find the Sisters of Solace, for they would tell us what we must do next," replied Livi, who did not ask how Dillon knew what was on her mind. Many times in the past Dillon listened to Livi in her sleep and regularly had a question ready for her when she awoke. He was pleased to hear the advice Livi had received in her dream for he knew the

Sisters of Solace were powers for good and there were too few of those in these troubled times.

"That should not be too difficult, provided they are where we expect to find them," added the dog.

After a breakfast of biscuits, which Livi complained about because it was too dry, they prepared themselves for the next leg of their journey. Dillon had considered seeking out more welcoming provision but had dismissed the notion. Foraging for food would have meant dropping their guard and there was no telling what creature might have penetrated this part of the kingdom now that Yksboor no longer protected its borders.

"How horrible must that be for a free spirit to be imprisoned against his will, tormented by the knowledge that the souls he had sworn to protect now lay bare to the wanton savagery of evil," Dillon thought to himself.

Soon they would have to find the Sisters of Solace.

Chapter 3

Deep in the darkest cavern, where no light pierced, a soul stirred. But though there was breath in the body the breathing was shallow, like the faintest wind blowing from far off. There was no real light in the eyes, just the faint clunk of chain-mail armour the only sound to be heard besides the laboured drawing of air in and out of tired lungs. Yksboor lay there, his spirit broken and his mind wandering. He felt helpless and hopeless and had long given up struggling against his bonds. His wrists were red raw and bloody where he had tried, and failed, for hours to break free. His mind was wandering and he was punishing himself for what he saw as his miserable and abject failure to carry out his avowed task. No thought gave he to the fact that the foe he had challenged had slain every brave soul that had come up against her. At the behest of her mistress, the witch known as Lady Half-Trousers, the dragon Tremgara had ravaged many parts of the kingdom until Yksboor had been drawn into a bloody fight. He had suspected at the time it was a trap and despite his foreboding had risen to the challenge. It gave him no comfort now that he had been proven right. He knew he had no choice other than to fight the dragon because his sworn task was to protect the people; his honour would not allow him to shirk the responsibility even though he knew in his heart he was probably riding to his death.

His beloved horse Celeste had been slain early in the battle when Tremgara had sprung the trap.

It had seemed so easy as he had followed her mistress's plan to the letter. Tremgara's daughter, Raygon, had lain in wait until Yksboor had been drawn into thinking he could strike a fatal blow to Tremgara. Her unexpected attack caught the knight off guard and he was knocked unconscious by the ferocity of her assault. When he awoke he was being dragged from the field of battle, the last thing he saw was the prone body of his loyal friend Celeste lying in a bloody pool before exhaustion again claimed him to a deep sleep.

The next thing he knew he was being awoken by a piercing screech which reached the very depths of his soul and which would have left any weaker soul cowering like a frightened child. He had long given up hope of any thoughts of rescue but, in truth, his own salvation now concerned him little. What darkened his mood was the thought of the witch and her beasts wreaking havoc upon the people he had sworn on forfeit of his own life to protect.

"I see you are awake, brave knight," the words spoken in a mocking tone and delivered in a cloud of steaming breath.

Yksboor looked up to where the sound came from, now facing the entrance to the cave which had become his prison. Lying across the entrance, eyeing him hungrily, was Raygon.

"Don't worry, I won't eat you, not yet anyway," snarled the dragon.

"My mother won't let me kill you until she has spoken to the witch."

The word was delivered with a note of contempt which Yksboor could not fail to recognise.

"I don't do anything to anger my mother, and nor will I. Not least until I can take her place," added the dragon, only in a much quieter tone, as if she feared the older dragon or one of her many allies might be within earshot.

"So what do you intend for me?" asked Yksboor, his body still sore from the bruises he had suffered when the dragons had fought him and dragged his limp body back to their lair.

"We will see. Maybe we will just kill you, and eat you as well. Maybe we will just keep you as a pet and play with you when the fancy takes us. My mother loves tormenting you mere mortals."

With that Raygon closed her eyes and gave the impression she was sleeping. But, as Yksboor knew only too well, the only dragon you could trust was one that was no longer breathing. He decided to make the most of his situation by sleeping himself, seeking respite from his sufferings, his aching body and his throbbing head.

Chapter 4

Harriet Paige and Emelia May, or Hattie and Millie as everyone knew them, were something of an enigma. They had lived together in peace for many years since their parents had been forced to flee. But rather than leave with the rest of the fleeing people when an invading army had swept through the land, the sisters had chosen to hide and would not leave their place of safety, not even when their parents came searching for them one last time. Instead they had known, and known without having to be told, that they had a purpose in life and that purpose was to remain and look after all the creatures of the forest where they lived, be the creatures human or otherwise. They were known by most as the sisters, but very few knew them as the Sisters of Solace. They had been given that name by a very wise and very old man. So old, in fact, that nobody remembered his name. They were the Sisters of Solace because that was what they provided. They either sought out the lost and injured or those without clear direction were drawn inexorably towards them. And once in their care the sisters never failed to protect. Even when the most evil and foul creatures were chasing them the pursued were always safe once they were under the protection of these two little girls. And apart from a little bit of mischief which dwelled within Millie's heart, they were good, and Millie always had Hattie to watch over her and make sure she did what was right.

It was with glad hearts that Dillon and Livi entered the forest where the Sisters of Solace lived. Livi had told Dillon that was what they should be called and also their given names, again the information having been given to her by her mother, not spoken but passed on as if without word. Dillon did not question how Livi knew, he just knew she knew and that was good enough reason for him.

It was then Dillon realised something wasn't quite right, something didn't quite feel how he knew it should feel. It was then he realised what it was – he could sense they were being watched as they walked between the leafy branches of the trees. Livi hadn't noticed, or so he thought, too busy bending down to pick wild flowers.

"Dillon," said Livi.

"Yes my princess," he replied.

"Don't worry about them, I know they are there and I will make them go away," she said, an air of understated confidence in her voice.

The peace was broken by a blood-curdling scream as several men, their bodies painted in dark colours and wrapped in animal skins, appeared all around them and started waving an assortment of weapons – swords, clubs and spears were but a few of them which could easily be recognised or described. As the men shouted and wailed there was no sound from Livi and Dillon stood his ground and started to growl, looking around to select his victim. Before Dillon could pounce the men dropped their weapons. They turned tail and ran as if frightened almost to death by a ferocious animal. Their faces were contorted in pain and from their mouths came cries of fear.

"See, I told you," said Livi cockily. "I just have to will it and bad things can do me no harm."

Dillon didn't really know how Livi was able to shape things to her will, she just was. And very lucky for them it was that she was able to do that too.

The danger averted, Livi and Dillon turned back to their journey for they still had a long way to go yet and neither had travelled this way before. Even though they felt safe in the knowledge they could protect themselves and were headed to meet the Sisters of Solace they were still burdened by the doubt which faces all travellers who are taking a journey for the first time. Not knowing how long the trip will take always nags away at a traveller, and Livi and Dillon were no different. Not until they reached their destination, which for now would take them to the Sisters of Solace, would they be able to relax and drop their guard.

Livi thought longingly of hot chocolate and sleep; Dillon thought of bones, sleep and chasing rabbits, which he would probably do later as he wagged his paws and lay stretched out in front of a roaring fire.

Just when they thought the journey would never end a young girl appeared on the road in front of them, a pretty little girl with an elfish grin.

"Who are you, and why are you here?" asked the girl of the two companions. As the first girl finished speaking another, older, girl appeared at her side.

"Take no notice of Millie. She knows who you are, both of you, and she knows why you are here. You've come looking for Yksboor," she said.

"I'm Hattie, by the way, and you're very welcome. If you've come to the aid of the brave knight then we are duty bound to help you. These lands have been a desperate place since he was taken from us by those dragons, I hate the foul beasts."

Livi and Dillon followed the sisters through the trees until they came to what looked like a vertical wall of green, with no apparent way through. Livi and Dillon looked on as the sisters walked towards the solid wall, but just as it appeared that they would walk into the wall and bounce off, they were able to walk straight through it.

As they disappeared through the wall, Millie turned and said, "Don't be silly, just follow us through. It's easy, you won't be hurt."

Once through the wall Livi and Dillon were inside a wide hallway.

"Don't worry, it's perfectly safe here, no harm can ever come to you when you are under our protection," said Hattie.

Dillon was the first to notice the smell and he was soon licking his lips. Livi smelled it almost at the same time, but not quite, as she very well knew, and as he regularly reminded her, Dillon's sense of smell was much better than hers. He had told her so on numerous occasions, so many times in fact that she could not even begin to recall how many.

"It's stew, vegetable stew," said Hattie.

"We don't eat animals here as we are sworn to protect them. If your dog wants meat he will have to go outside to hunt and eat. But I warn you, once he is outside he is beyond our protection."

"It's okay, vegetable stew will suffice," said Dillon, the memory of a breakfast of biscuits still clear in his mind and on his tastebuds.

After a hearty dinner of vegetable stew, followed by strawberries with cream, and washed down with homemade lemonade, Livi plucked up the courage to ask several questions which had been occupying her mind.

"Where are your parents?" asked Livi.

"We don't know. They fled with everyone else when the evil men came to his land," said Hattie.

"We don't know if we will ever see them again. We hope we will, we live in hope, but we don't know for certain. Why do you ask?"

"It just seemed strange two girls like you living in the forest, looking after yourselves," replied Livi.

"And not only that, you care for anyone that comes this way and keep them safe from evil."

Hattie shrugged her shoulders, a tear appearing in the corner of one eye. As she wiped it away with the back of her hand, she said: "It's just what we do. We hope our parents will find us but we are happy to do what we do, it fills our hearts with joy that we can help people. Our payment is their smiles."

The newly found friends talked for a long time until the fire became very low and they retired to their beds. Livi and Dillon shared a very large bed in one of the bedrooms off the main chamber, the young girl dreaming of her mummy and the dog off to chase some rabbits.

Livi woke the next morning to find she was alone. A moment of panic filled her heart and she felt a lump in her throat. She ran out into the chamber but was greeted by the sound of a dog barking and the shrieks of an excited child.

"Chase me Dillon, chase me," Millie was shouting as she stood in one of the doorways.

But just as Dillon appeared around the corner and ran to where Millie had been the young girl was gone, leaving a trail of bright light behind her as she appeared to be spirited away. The fun went on for several seconds and soon Livi lost interest in Dillon's fruitless pursuit of Millie. He was obviously having great fun and Livi felt it was very harsh of her to think about trying to stop him. She decided to leave him and his new friend to it and she went to see where Hattie was. She found her in the kitchen, busy mixing something in a bowl.

"There's porridge if you want it, and honey too," said Hattie.

"I couldn't," said Livi. "I'm still full from last night, I ate enough to feed an army."

"It's always wise to take food when it's offered in these parts, you never know when you will eat again, particularly a hot meal," said Hattie. "I will pack you up some food for the onward journey," she added.

Livi said nothing, lost in thoughts of what the journey ahead held in store for them. She turned away and went in search of her dog who was still filling the place with loud barks to match the laughter of Millie. Turning a corner Livi was nearly knocked off her feet as Dillon came bowling down the corridor in front of her. Just in the nick of time, Dillon skidded to a halt and leaned his paws on Livi's shoulders, licking her face excitedly.

"That's enough Dillon, I'm not a baby bird any more," exclaimed Livi as she held the dog far enough away that his licking tongue was just out of reach of her face.

A short while later Livi and Dillon were ready to continue their journey. Hattie had given them directions on how to reach their next destination, The Hanging Pole, and also given them a bag of provisions. Livi had long wondered why it was called The Hanging Pole, and now she had learned. It was where an evil lord hanged the people he didn't care for, and some he had stopped caring for.

The only thing that warmed Livi's heart was the knowledge she had gained from the sisters which had confirmed the purpose of the journey. The fondness with which the sisters had spoken of Yksboor had told Livi all she needed to know. She and Dillon had to rescue Yksboor.

Chapter 5

The Hanging Pole had only one purpose. It started life as a tree and it had long since stopped being used as shelter for the animals of the forest, or as a perch for birds, or a home for squirrels. Stripped of its branches and bark, all that was left was the bare trunk of a tree with a pulley fixed to the top and a rope running over the pulley. Near the base was a hook where the rope secured and the unfortunate were left to die. Unfortunate, because they had incurred the wrath of the lord who held power for as far as the human eye could see, and further. For some their crime was no more than to be caught looking at the lord or one of his six wives. He had six wives – all of them younger than him and very pretty – because he deserved at least one day off a week, one day when he could just be by himself.

Many had met their end at The Hanging Pole, left to die and left to provide sustenance for the crows and other carrion which came upon their lifeless bodies.

Livi didn't want to go to The Hanging Pole but she knew she had to seek out the evil lord. He would be able to tell her where she could find Yksboor but she knew she would have to trade for that information. It wasn't something she was looking forward to, but nevertheless, it was something she had to face.

Thankfully The Hanging Pole wasn't occupied when Livi and Dillon eventually arrived there. Then there was nothing for them to do but wait. Sooner or later the next unfortunate victim would be dragged to the pole to meet his or her fate. The minutes passed like hours but there was at last a sound down the pathway. Dillon heard it first – his superior hearing again – but it wasn't long after that Livi also heard the sound. The companions strained their eyes until a small group of people came slowly into view. The group was four strong – three men in black and a young boy bound in chains and shackles and being led by a rope which was tied around his neck. The only sound that could be heard was a whimpering noise coming from the mouth of the boy, tears washing down his grubby face.

As they got closer the boy forced a smile but the three guards took no notice as they didn't expect a small girl and her dog to cause them any bother. As they got closer Livi stood up from where she had been sitting patiently on the ground and Dillon adopted a threatening pose as he rose on to all four legs.

One of the guards stopped and surveyed the young girl and the dog, neither of them looking particularly fierce or threatening.

"Them two, what you think they up to?" he asked his companions.

"Pay them no heed until we've done what we have to do," said the tallest of the three.

"Then we'll tie them up and take them back to our master, a pretty penny he will pay for them so I'm sure a fine ransom they will fetch," he added, grinning approvingly and letting a wicked grin pass across his scarred and pock-marked face.

Dillon stiffened, sensing a change in the body language of the three men surrounding the boy. Before anyone could move Livi had focused her gaze on the boy's three captors. The next thing they knew they were being forced to their knees even though no one was near them except for the boy. Not only were they unable to move but their minds were also filled with unexplainable fear.

Livi walked towards them and took the rope which was around the boy's neck. Quietly she removed it from around his neck and tossed it aside, leading him by the hand to where Dillon stood keeping guard.

"Don't be afraid, you're safe now," she said to the boy.

"What's your name?" she asked.

"William," he replied.

"Hello William, I'm Livi and the handsome dog is called Dillon."

Then she turned her gaze to the three men, paralysed by fear and trembling, unable to move and even unable to utter a single word.

"I desire to speak with your master. Tell him I have denied him what he derives most pleasure from, what he considers his right, the right to take someone's life. Now, be gone and deliver my message to your master."

With that the three men were released from their invisible bonds and were able to rise from their knees.

For a fleeting moment they thought about attacking the girl and the dog, their pride wounded by being subjugated by one so small and delicate.

The same thought had crossed Livi's mind and her steely gaze and the fire in her eyes paralysed them again, if only for an instant, and they turned on their heels and fled the scene.

"That should bring him here, if he can get a sensible word out of any of them," said Dillon with a growl.

"The dog... he talked," said William, an incredulous look on his face as he pointed at Dillon.

"Yes he does, have you never heard a dog talk before?" asked Livi.

"No, never, wait till I tell my ma and pa. They won't believe me, or me brothers and sisters."

Livi waited for the excited look to leave the boy's eyes and, after checking out his dishevelled appearance, explained what must happen next before the evil lord arrived.

"Go now with Dillon, he will keep you safe and out of harm's way," said Livi.

"Come, do as she says," said Dillon as he led the way into the nearest clump of bushes.

Half an hour later a group of men came riding along on horses. At their head was a heavy, thick-set giant of a man on a white horse, his face covered with a thick beard the colour of which matched his dark black hair, and a scowl across his face.

The men, six of them and all on large mounts, pulled up and then circled their charges around where Livi sat.

The girl didn't flinch, instead she kept her gaze fixed ahead and didn't move at all or blink her eyes once.

Eventually the leader of the men, who Livi knew was the one she sought, pulled up his horse. The other men followed suit and copied his stance as he leant forward in his saddle, the reins held loosely in one hand.

"What do we have here?" he boomed.

Then he answered his own question.

"A girl who defies me. I must admit you have spirit, a spirit I shall enjoy breaking. And I'm going to take my time over my sport."

With this the whole group burst into laughter.

"How are you going to entertain us? I hear tell you can bend the minds of men to your will. So, how will you do that? Come, don't be shy, I like you to show me."

"Maybe I should sing a song for you," suggested Livi.

"Why not. Sing us a song and then I will make you dance to my tune," said the evil lord, a wicked grin spread across his face.

Livi opened her mouth and began to sing.

Immediately Dillon's ears pricked up as he took shelter in the nearby clump of bushes and the young boy just stared in wonderment.

But just as Livi's song brought gladness to the hearts of good people it brought pain and agony to those whose hearts were given to hatred.

At the same time as Livi's song brought smiles to the faces of Dillon and William it brought anguish and fear to the faces of the seven horsemen. It got so unbearable that they released their grip on the reins of their horses and clasped their hands over their eyes.

Unnervingly, for the horsemen, their horses seemed unaffected.

"Make it stop, make it stop," demanded the evil lord in a commanding voice.

"Say please, didn't your mummy ever teach you to say please," said Livi in a dismissive voice.

"Please, please, make it stop," he replied.

Livi ceased singing and fixed the lord with a determined stare.

"Would you like me to start singing again or should I name my terms?" enquired Livi.

"So what are these terms? I wonder," came his reply.

"I need to know where the knight is being held. And, what's more, I want one of your men to guide me there."

"The knight, what's he to you? He's better dead and, where he is, he will be dead very soon, perhaps sooner rather than later."

"Just tell me how to find him and we will forget about the guide," snapped an impatient Livi.

"Why should I tell you where he is? If he escapes, which I don't consider possible, he will only come back and spoil the fun my men and I have had since he was taken by the dragons. What is he to you?"

"My family owes him a debt of gratitude. You could ignore my request but I don't think you want me singing again, do you?"

Reluctantly the lord turned and spoke to one of his men, sighing in resignation before asking a question and listening intently to the answer. He turned his gaze back to Livi and started to speak.

He gave directions in the form of a story explaining how the mother dragon had begun her life and terrorised people up and down the land. As the story unfolded Livi was able to commit a picture in her mind, a map of the journey she and Dillon must take.

"What of the boy?" asked the lord.

"He goes with me," replied Livi.

"One day you may be in my grasp and I will make you pay for this," said the evil lord, clearly agitated at being frustrated by a small girl and her dog.

"I look forward to singing you another song," replied Livi.

She watched the group of men for a couple of minutes before they turned their horses away and rode slowly down the path before their mounts broke into a trot and then a gallop.

"You can come out now," said Livi after the horsemen had disappeared from sight.

Dillon trotted over and sat obediently by her side. William walked over and looked at Livi, an uncertain gaze on his face. She could see he was not sure what to do or even to think about what he had seen.

"What becomes of me?" he asked.

"Well. You can remain here and wait for the lord and his henchmen to come back or you can join us. Turn our little party into three and come along for the ride."

"Why not? I've nothing to lose, I just hope I don't spoil everything for you. I always seem to do the wrong thing, everyone is always telling me I'm clumsy. That's why I ended up here."

"Why? What happened?" asked Livi.

"I spilt some wine. The lord wasn't happy; it was his favourite wine and the last in the bottle. He said I had to be severely punished. He wanted me to share in his disappointment," he said.

"No one will punish you, I won't allow it. You are safe for as long as you are with me."

The three new friends looked at each other and then started walking down the path, Livi leading the way and Dillon bringing up the rear, keeping his wits about him and remaining alert to any danger that might present itself along the way.

As they walked, Livi was lost in thought. She knew many dangers lay ahead of them and the uncertainty of what was to come made her unhappy. She had a clear image of their route in her head but she had little real idea of what foul beasts and ill-meaning men would show themselves along the way, trying with everything they had to prevent Livi and her companions from getting to where they must go.

Chapter 6

Slowly he awoke, his mind foggy and his thoughts confused. How long he had been asleep he did not know, whether he would ever get out of this horrible place was something he gave little thought to. All he could think of was how he had let himself be captured and how with every second he was failing in his sworn duty to protect the people of the kingdom. There could be no pain keener than that which he felt because he was not doing the duty that he took every breath to fulfil. Nothing seemed to appear clear in his mind no matter how hard he tried to concentrate. And yet through his confused mind he could see that something was not quite the same. Something was different. He lay there motionless and tried to think clearly. What made it worse was the awful smell, a foul and acrid stink which burned his nose and throat. Slowly it dawned on him what had changed. There was no dragon guarding him.

He raised his head slowly from where he lay on the damp ground, surveying the cave which had been his prison for how long he did not know. Was it days? Maybe weeks even? He just didn't know. That only increased his sense of despair as he could have been in that hole for weeks, making him even more desperate to get back to what he should be doing: protecting the innocent. After lying there thinking what to do, his mind wracked with uncertainty over what course of action he had to follow, he finally decided action had to be taken.

The entrance to the cave stank of these foul beasts and the smell was so strong it made Yksboor want to gag and he had to wait a moment to catch his breath as the cool fresh air of the outside finally won its battle with the filthy fog he had been forced to breathe during his period of captivity. After catching his breath he knew he had to try to make his bid for freedom. He knew it had been too easy, that the dragons weren't that careless, but the burning desire to do his duty far outweighed any thoughts of self-preservation.

The instant he broke the cover of the cave all the questions he had asked himself about his escape bid were answered.

Like a thunderbolt the scream pierced the calm of the day. The whole ground shook as Yksboor made his bid to reach the cover of the trees across the clearing. Wind blew across the clearing and it swept Yksboor off his feet. The wind came from the beating wings of the dragons as they circled the clearing. In turn they swooped down from the sky, scorching the treetops with a blast of flame from their nostrils. If Yksboor could have seen their faces he would have realised they were smiling. But he was far too busy trying to dodge the wind created by their beating wings, trying desperately to get back onto his feet so he could run away. But each time he managed to get to his feet down swooped one of the dragons to knock him down again with a beat of their powerful wings. This went on for half an hour, Yksboor getting no nearer his escape and the dragons slowly getting bored with their game. Eventually Yksboor lay motionless on the ground as the dragons landed and walked over to his prone body.

"So, true knight, did you really think we would let you escape?" asked Tremgara. "Do you like our little game?"

"Yes, it was rather clever of me to come up with it, wasn't it mother," said Raygon.

Tremgara's gaze turned from her prey towards her daughter and the younger dragon instantly knew she had made a mistake. She looked sheepishly away as Tremgara returned her gaze to the fallen knight. She walked over and placed her clawed foot on the knight's chest.

"Let's get our little plaything back where he belongs and then you can make sure he doesn't think about escaping ever again, can't you my dear."

"Yes mother," replied Raygon.

Yksboor knew there could be no desperation darker than that which he now felt. He was at the mercy of the two dragons and saw no way of escaping. Dark thoughts clouded his mind; maybe he would be better if he was released from his duty once and for all, so that he didn't feel so keenly that he had failed everyone. Tremgara curled her claws around his body and lifted him up, tossing him across the clearing and into the mouth of the cave.

"Stay there, and don't you dare think about trying to escape again or I'll let Raygon eat you, as she's been begging me ever since we captured you."

As he lay there in the entrance to the cave a thought came to Yksboor. If they wanted to kill him they would have done it a long time ago. No, they wanted him alive but didn't want him free. Even in his confused mind he realised what was going on. The dragons wanted to lure someone else here who would try to help him escape. That was their plan. A plan he wouldn't let them put into practice. No. He would bide his time and make himself stronger again so that he would be best served to stop their evil scheme bearing its poisoned fruit.

Chapter 7

The Queen sat alone staring from her balcony across the land over which she reigned. In the far distance she could see the black plumes of smoke snaking their way into the sky. Signs of the advance of evil, be it wild men or those foul dragon beasts, which was spreading across the land. In her hands she held a message from her son, Prince Nathan, which more than asked for her presence, it almost demanded it. The question of Nathan's disobedience had long vexed her. She had thought his decision to fight in the far-off war would teach him discipline and a pure heart but whatever responsibility he had taken on it had seemed to do little to moderate his selfish attitude. Should she acquiesce? After all, one day he would take over as ruler and she would be under his command. For several hours she had studied the message requiring her presence in Baithwaite. Even for Nathan it appeared something was not quite right, but it was written in his own hand and signed with his name.

"I must obey, I have no choice," she said, almost a whisper.

Chapter 8

Hattie and Millie were busy picking mushrooms when Hattie suddenly stopped, her nose twitching. She knew that smell, she thought: evil was in the forest.

"What are you doing, why have you stopped picking?" enquired Millie.

Hattie ignored her sister's questions and appeared lost in deep thought. After what seemed like an age Hattie gently knelt down beside her sister and told her young sibling, in a quiet voice only just louder than a whisper, what she must do.

"Millie," she said. "There's evil about in the forest. Don't worry because we shall always be safe from it. But we must warn others of what is happening. I need you to go to the Queen and tell her. Tell her that we saw her daughter, the princess, and her dog and that they were both safe and well when they left us. You must tell her that evil has since entered the forest. Tell her to take all caution, and tell the people to take shelter and guard against strangers."

Hattie knew that Millie would be safe because she could run faster than the wind. When she had played with Dillon earlier, play was what she had been about. If she had been serious about wanting to evade Dillon the dog would not have seen her let alone have any hope of catching up with her.

Millie carefully handed her basket to Hattie, hugged her sister and then they said their goodbyes. With that the young girl was gone as if in a flash of magic.

Hattie was left alone to worry about her sister, for worrying was Hattie's station in life after she had taken responsibility for both of them since they had been separated from their parents. Hattie didn't have long to stand and think, though, because she heard noises far off in the forest. The evil was approaching, she had smelled them and now she heard them and she knew it wouldn't be long before she saw them too. She had better take cover.

From her perch high in a tree Hattie could see far down the forest path. She knew from which direction they were coming and she knew they would do bad things to her if they caught her.

She had chosen a tall tree which provided plenty of cover but also afforded her a good view. The noises of the men, if that was what they were, were getting closer and closer. Hattie had watched the creatures which normally inhabited this part of the forest either scamper away or take refuge in holes or in the deep cover of vegetation.

Eventually she saw them come into view. An evil band of men dressed in bloody battle-torn clothing and not a handsome one among them. Many wore the scars of battle on their faces and arms or even their bare chests, showing off with pride that they weren't afraid to get hurt as they pillaged and plundered their way through life. At their head was the evil lord, he of the 'Hanging Pole' who had people killed for sport.

Hattie had never seen men up close and nor did she choose to. Hopefully they would be gone soon and she could slip quietly back to her home. But then Hattie's heart sank as she watched as the lord halted his horse and dismounted.

"This will do," he said. "We make camp here for the night. I want guards set. Anyone found skulking about here will meet their maker. And any man who captures that meddlesome girl and her dog will be richly rewarded."

'He must mean the princess and Dillon,' Hattie thought to herself. 'I do hope Millie gets back soon. I'm glad I told her to go straight home and wait for me there.'

Hattie knew the easiest and safest thing to do would be to wait for darkness and then slip away quietly. However, she desperately wanted to find out what these men were up to. She would have to wait for cover of darkness and then sneak into their camp to find out.

The lord had waited patiently, from the moment he had seen the basket of flowers and mushrooms lying on the ground where it had been abandoned. He had given it much thought but decided against alerting his men. Many hours had passed but no thing and no person had shown itself. However, he was going nowhere, so he could afford to be patient and he was determined to win the waiting game. That girl had taken his sport from him and he was determined not to be cheated a second time. He wanted blood and nothing was going to prevent him getting his bloodlust sated.

Hattie had waited long enough, she decided, before she made her move. Carefully she made her way down from the tree where she was hiding. Most of the men were asleep, some from the effects of too much alcohol, but there were still some posted as guards and others sat around the fire for warmth. Slowly and, she thought, silently she made her way to a big oak tree near the camp fire. She stood against it and concentrated her hearing so that she could find out what they were doing in this part of the forest. But what she hadn't bargained on was that someone had been waiting for her, alert to the fact that she was close by. As she stood there in the darkness Hattie wasn't aware she was being observed.

The evil lord waited until he saw the person, for it was a person, was concentrating on the men around the fire before he allowed himself a silent chuckle, or one that was hardly audible for he didn't want to alert his prey to the fact that they had been discovered.

And then he pounced, deftly crossing the gap between himself and the tree where he grabbed his target by the shoulders and slipped a sack over their head.

"My, you struggle gamely, for a small one," said the startled lord.

"But don't struggle too hard or I shall be forced to crush you with my bare hands and that would spoil my fun, if not yours."

After struggling to get away a startled Hattie had given up her attempts to break free.

"What is it my lord?" exclaimed one of the men as they all left their places around the fire. Even the guards had abandoned their posts to see what was happening.

"Master, master, what ails you?" cried another.

"Nothing, come see what I have caught. We shall have our sport, of that I am sure. Come, bring me light," he replied.

One of the men took a torch and lit it in the fire before holding it aloft to illuminate the scene.

The evil lord removed the sack and almost lost his grip he was so amazed. Hattie felt his grip loosen and made her bid to break for freedom. But before she could get away his grip tightened like a vice as his right hand clamped itself on her shoulder, bruising the skin as his grip was so firm and his determination so resolute.

"A girl, a girl, what a surprise. But she struggles like a man, no a bear, she is so fierce."

"What's she doing here? What shall we do with her?" asked one of the startled men.

"She's no sport, we'll have to let her go," added another, a man of some authority judging by his attire, and a man of keen appetite judging by his girth.

He had obviously become complacent with the importance he had drawn from his own station. It took only one glance from his lord and master for the man to realise he had made a grave error of judgement. Although it was not a fatal mistake it was one he vowed silently never to repeat.

"No sport, no sport," boomed the lord as he cast an accusing glance at the man.

"I'll show you sport, but first I want to know what a girl is doing sneaking upon us," he added, a snarl leaving his lips like a baying animal when the scent of blood fills its nostrils.

Since he had been a young boy, when his father first took him hunting and had marked him with the blood of a deer which they had hunted on horse and brought down with bow and arrow, he had derived his greatest pleasure from inflicting pain upon others. The fact that his latest capture was a young girl made no real difference to him, he was going to enjoy this as he had done countless other times.

"Right girl, tell me why you are here," he demanded.

In response Hattie said nothing, silently cursing for allowing herself to be captured. Her mind was filled with the sharp pain of disappointment and also with the fast spreading fear of what her foolishness would mean for her sister. How would Millie look after herself without her big sister to protect her?

She had failed in her duty to look after her sister. Inwardly she allowed herself to cry as showing her feelings would be a sign of weakness her captors would feed upon voraciously. There was no way she would show weakness, no matter what they threatened or did to her, of that she was sure.

"Not very talkative, are we," said the lord. "No worry, I know how to make you squeal like a pig stuck on a pikestaff," he said as he locked his other hand around her neck and started to squeeze.

Hattie closed her eyes and started to think of nice things as she tried to block out the fear of an ever-increasing pain.

It was then that it happened, but those in the clearing had little idea of what was going on before it was over.

The next thing Hattie knew she was running through the forest, her hand held in Millie's as her sister, giggling, led the way. Hattie had little idea of what had happened but she was just mightily relieved she was now free. Eventually, for it seemed a long time later although, in reality, it was merely seconds, the sisters stopped running.

It was then Millie recounted her story to Hattie. Upon returning home Millie had waited as her sister had told her. She always did what she was told, she repeated parrot fashion, as she had done when she returned from her appointed task. After several hours of patiently waiting she had decided to go looking for Hattie and had gone back to where they had parted earlier in the day. It was then she came upon the scene of her sister's capture. It was a simple task for her to run swiftly through the camp and release Hattie, unlocking the vice-like grip that foul man had on her sister's neck and shoulder long before he realised what was happening. It was then Hattie remembered feeling the grip of her captor had been released and she found the waiting hand of her sister. As they stood there embracing there was another scene, far off in the forest, but that was not quite so peaceful. Angered to be cheated of his sport for a second time that day the lord had flown into an uncontrollable rage. He lashed out at any man close enough to be within the range of his flailing fists, bringing yelps of anguish and cries of pain from the fleeing soldiers. For many long minutes the men sought cover as the lord's desire for some recompense was wrought upon his helpless companions. For many days they would bear the bruises and scars of his wrath. Only those fortunate enough to evade him and find a safe place to hide for the night were spared the suffering his anger inflicted upon anyone caught up in his relentless assaults.

Now they were safe Hattie took a little time to check her shoulder and neck, where her probing fingers felt the bruises. But at least she was spared further pain and indignity.

"Right, Millie, homeward we go," said Hattie.

"How went your audience with the Queen?"

"Very well, thank you," replied Millie. "I told her we had seen her daughter and her dog, and of the capture of Yksboor by the dragons."

"What did she say?" asked Hattie.

"She said she feared for Yksboor and for the state of his mind if he was in the clutches of not one but two dragons. She was sure Livi and Dillon would be safe and that they would aid Yksboor in his bid to escape. The Queen has been called away by her son, though I think that is a duty she feels obliged rather than happy to fulfil."

The sisters turned and headed for home, following their instinct to take the correct path rather than use their bodily senses.

Chapter 9

Livi had heard many stories which included tell of 'The Tortured Path' as it was named. It was only when she had to take The Tortured Path herself that Livi fully appreciated the significance of the name. Enclosed by a wall of tall trees growing tightly together, the path had barely any space upon it for exposed green of grass or brown of dirt. Pointed rocks, scattered in a random pattern as if they had been picked up and thrown down with no real purpose, dotted the way and made the going slow and painful. For many miles Livi and Dillon, and their new companion William, had suffered a painful and difficult journey as they followed the directions given to them by the evil lord. More than once Livi had wondered whether she had been tricked with false witness of the way forward she should take. And yet she knew this way was the true way to the destination she sought because it was the most difficult route she had ever taken to get anywhere. More than once she thought how much easier it would have been to travel where they wanted to go if they had wings like a dragon, or the wings of a real dragon, to ease their burden. But that thought made her shudder as it would have meant capture by the foul beasts, a fate that had already befallen many before. A fate more miserable she couldn't imagine if she had been that unfortunate, or foolish, to allow it to befall her. With a weary sigh she turned her gaze to the faithful Dillon and the waif-like William. How good it had been for the boy to throw his lot in with them. An instant good judge of character, Livi had decided William was a worthy companion and one who would repay their faith in him with honesty and unstinting friendship.

Another hour into their journey, and still making slow progress on the straight but bumpy road, the three companions came upon a clearing to the side of the path. There they made camp for the night. They ate a little food, bread and cheese, but were unable to warm their bodies with the heat from a fire because Dillon had warned against it for fear their position would be given away by the smoke it would create. To make up for the lack of a fire or a warm bed, Livi had huddled up to Dillon and took warmth from the heat his body gave off, the beat of his heart a comfort as she allowed herself to be lost in the tranquillity and rejuvenating properties which sleep brought to her tired mind and body.

The next morning Livi woke to find she was alone in the clearing. Startled, she looked around quietly to see where Dillon and William had gone. Her questions were answered when Dillon came bounding up to her.

"Where have you been?" she questioned the panting dog.

"We went to look for food and water, and we found both. Look at what William has."

The boy stood before them with a pail, which he had carried in his backpack, filled with water. In his other hand he held mushrooms and herbs. These he dropped into the pail which he placed on the ground as he set about building up a small pile of sticks and other kindling. He took a tinder box from his backpack and lit the fire. He explained, as he worked, that he would only let it burn long enough to boil the soup. After a breakfast of mushroom and herb soup, together with bread from their provisions, the trio, who were much refreshed, returned to their tiresome journey. The only thing that kept Livi focused on the way forward was the knowledge that she would be fighting for a good cause when they finally arrived at their destination, the dragon's lair. Livi had long hated dragons, having witnessed the aftermath of their wrath and also been told the time-honoured tales of their wanton destruction by her mother. This journey, long and arduous, had done nothing to improve her opinion of the scaly creatures. But that was a battle for another day, for this day at least she concentrated on placing one foot in front of the other.

Another day of travel and the weary companions settled down to sleep once more. William, tired and sore, was soon fast asleep. Livi and Dillon talked about what had happened so far on their journey and what possibly lay ahead.

"I know you trust your gut feeling, always going with what feels right, but something bothers me about the boy," said Dillon. "I know I should trust your judgement as I always do, and invariably it is right. But I can't help feeling something just doesn't add up and I don't like it. I'm worried by something and I can't tell what it is."

"I know, I feel it too, but I'm not sure what it is either," added Livi.

"When you look at the circumstances in which we found him and the fact he has agreed to come with us on our perilous journey we can't take any action without having any proof to back up our feelings."

As they talked William lay on his side with his back to them. He was awake and he was sure they were talking about him. He didn't need to hear their words to know they had doubts about him. He was wracked with doubt but the thought of what might happen to his parents was the only thing that filled his pained mind. He didn't like doing what he knew he must do, not one little bit, but he had no choice. It was like he had been told by the old dragon, he would follow orders and lead the girl and the dog into the trap or he would be made to watch his parents being torn limb from limb.

The friends had been travelling for what seemed like days, if not a week, and they were all growing tired and weary.

Livi's thoughts turned to home, dreaming of all the love she missed so much and she hoped the road would end soon.

William's thoughts were not of love, but of pain, the pain he was feeling intensely inside his head as his conscience fought with his duty towards his parents. If only he could check that his parents were safe from the clutches of the evil lord and he could be free to help his new-found friends. 'What am I to do?' he thought to himself.

While Livi and William focussed on things far off it was as well that Dillon's mind was here and in the present as danger was just about to rear its ugly countenance once more in an otherwise peaceful land.

Dillon was tense, his body stiff like a board, as his nose pointed in the direction of approaching danger and a snarl started to appear on his face and his lip slowly started to curl upwards to show his clenched teeth.

Livi and William realised something was wrong at exactly the same moment and looked in the same direction as the dog. Nothing came into view down the path but they could hear the noise of approaching footfalls. Quickly and without sound they left the path upon which they had only recently resumed walking and sought the shelter of some nearby bushes. After what seemed like an eternity the evil lord rode into view, his men running behind and struggling to keep up as they laboured under the heavy burden of their equipment and provisions. Something bothered Livi about the scene and then it came to her. As if by some magic these men were able to run on the path where Livi and her companions had struggled to walk. A spell, no doubt, had been used. Livi studied the scene and, for once, her brain struggled to formulate a new plan with which to outwit their foe. Dillon was only thinking about one thing, running straight into the oncoming soldiers and fighting it out. Before either of them could do anything they noticed William was no longer at their side. They realised too late what he was doing when they saw him stood in the middle of the path, his arms folded and his feet apart in a display of defiance no one could mistake. As he stood there William wasn't feeling as brave as he had when he had come up with this bright idea. He had won the battle inside his head and his conscience had told him to protect his new friends. Now he wasn't so sure what he had decided to do was such a good idea and the thought again of the peril he might be placing his parents in. But it was too late, he had to face up to what he must do. The one thing that kept coming back into his head was what his father had told him, the one pearl of wisdom he had always known he would put to use one day.

"The avoidance of combat is an art form." That was what his father had said. It had always mystified him but William now knew it was the only way he would be able to beat such a determined enemy, and one so well armed and supported by such a retinue.

"Well, what's it to be then?" asked the lord as he reined in his horse.

"Are you keeping your half of the bargain or do I get to have some sport with your snivelling parents? Come on, quickly now, I haven't got all day and there's some sport to be had, I can smell it and it's an aroma I have come to love down the years."

The lord could not contain his excitement. The dragon had told him what the witch commanded. The boy, under threat of harm to his parents, would lead the girl and the dog to their capture by the dragons. And that would bring the prince and the Queen running. Then they would have them all safely captured and could do as they pleased throughout the land.

"The avoidance of combat is an art form," said the small boy.

The smile which had broken across the lord's face was replaced by a scowl.

"I don't know what that means but it sounds to me like a challenge. Have at you."

As the lord lunged out with his sword he realised too late that the lunge had missed its target. The boy had deftly moved aside and had also leapt onto the back of the horse behind the lord and flipped his tunic over his head, taking a rope and looping it around the neck of his assailant, tying it with a knot. As he jumped to the ground he kicked out with his foot into the side of the horse which resulted in the mount bolting off down the track with the startled rider on top. The men looked on in bewilderment at the scene, some trying to follow the course of the horse while the rest were intent on harming the source of their master's discomfort. The startled cries of the lord as he was carried off down the path made their minds up for all of the men.

"The avoidance of combat," said William as he watched the men running after their lord.

Livi and Dillon broke cover and went straight up to William. Livi wasn't happy and her displeasure was shared by the dog who was contemplating giving the boy a piece of his mind, at the very least.

"We heard that, all of it. What's going on?" asked Livi.

William kept his face pointed to the ground, as much that Livi and Dillon couldn't see the tears in his eyes as if to hide the shame he felt.

He blurted out: "They had my parents. They told me that if I didn't do as they said and lead you into a trap where dragons would lie in wait that they would kill both my parents, slowly and painfully, while I was forced to watch. I, to my shame, had agreed to do it but I couldn't go through with it. I hope you can forgive me. I want to help you, I want to defy that man, but I am so scared that harm will come to my parents. I want to go to them and warn them but I feel I should not abandon you to your fate. For not only are there dragons about but also a witch, and she, I am told, is the wickedest of them all. I don't know what I should do," added William, as he began to cry uncontrollably.

"What you did here was a very brave thing," said Livi.

"For that alone we are in your debt and therefore I say you should go to your parents. They need you and you should make sure they are safe. I am sure that even Dillon agrees with me there," said the girl as she gave her faithful companion a sideways look.

"Aye, I agree, although I wasn't so sure when I heard what that rogue was saying to the young lad," said Dillon.

"Go then, it is decided, and find your parents. Dillon and I shall be fine, even though the way will be treacherous and full of peril. And go with our blessing," added Livi.

Livi and Dillon watched as the boy turned away from them and began to trot down the path in the opposite direction from that which the startled horse was still carrying the lord with all of his men trailing in his wake.

"So we are two again, sweet princess, and the happier I am for it," said Dillon.

"I know why you feel that way, particularly as William joined us with bad intent," replied Livi.

"But he had reason. I don't know what I would do if someone I loved faced such peril. If my mother or brother was in such danger it would question my resolve. The good thing about William, his saving grace, was that he chose right despite the fact it could place those he loved in danger and the torment that knowledge would put him through. He is fair and kind of heart and for that we should be thankful and release him to do his duty to his parents. For us, a different path lies ahead. The road will be difficult, and fraught with peril, but we must take it and face all that comes our way with stout hearts and steady resolve."

Chapter 10

Yksboor stirred once again from a deep but painful sleep. Waking up felt like a long, slow and tortured climb up never-ending steps. The knight lay for long moments as he tried to gather his thoughts. He so desperately wanted to rise to his feet, fight and slay the dragon guarding him and then return to his sworn oath of protecting the people of this land. But he knew he could not fight his way to freedom in his current state. He tried to search his mind to discover why he felt so drowsy. Was there some trickery being used to hold his mind? Or was his mind just broken by what he had gone through? It would be some time yet before he was ready to make his bid for freedom, he had been beaten and bruised the last time when he had been drawn into making his escape bid before his mind and body were up to the task.

The dragon, which lay in the entrance to the cave, opened one eye and fixed the knight with a fierce gaze.

"Ah, you're awake now, at long last," said Raygon. "You've slept for days since my mother put you in your place. She's away on business and left me to be your gaoler. Please, please, try to escape and give me the slightest excuse to burn you to a cinder! Look, good sir knight, please make a break for freedom. Then it will be goodnight, good knight," said Raygon, the words followed by a horrible cackle and a blast of fire which burnt the branches off the trees around the entrance to the cave.

Yksboor turned away from the dragon and tried to close his eyes. But as he lay there he could hear what he recognised as the bleating of a sheep or goat. He turned towards where the dragon lay so he could see what was happening. The scene before him filled him with dread. Before him several creatures led a goat into the clearing outside the cave and tethered the cowering animal to a post before running off into the trees like so many frightened rabbits. It took what appeared to be an eternity before the dragon rose to its feet and stretched out its long neck. With a quick movement the dragon swallowed the goat, the rope which had tethered the animal dangling from the beast's mouth. Yksboor shielded his ears as he heard the bones of the goat crunch as it was eaten alive.

'There is no way, in all conscience, I can allow one more creature to suffer such a fate,' Yksboor thought to himself.

Slowly he drifted off into a fitful sleep, hoping in vain that he could regain his strength so he could escape and return from this torment to his oath of duty.

Chapter 11

Many miles away the prince mopped his heavily sweating brow as he sat uneasily on his horse, its head bowed in weariness from what had felt like endless toil.

Nathan surveyed the scene before him and the fact that the forces loyal to him had prevailed did not fill him with any sense of achievement or happiness. All about him across the fields lay man and beast, motionless and no longer drawing breath. The two armies had battled long and hard, through the heat of the day and until dark had nearly fallen. As the triumphant force, Nathan's army was mopping up what remained of the forces allied to the witch in a series of bloody skirmishes. True, the battle had been won but it was far from a decisive victory. And the greater damage had been done to the forces of the young prince as many men and horses had been slaughtered or injured. Their opponents had been driven from the battlefield but they would be back, reinforced and reinvigorated by the witch who would use all of her guile and knowledge to make sure she could redouble her efforts to batter the forces of good into submission until she added this Kingdom to her ever-growing domain.

"Sire, sire, I bring news," said a horseman as he rode up to the prince and his captains.

"My liege, an army approaches. Many men and beasts, not more than a day's march from here."

Nathan turned to Roger, his trusted general, and looked his closest friend straight in the eyes.

"We must leave this place," he said.

"Gather every man and every horse, those that can ride and those that can walk, leave the badly wounded behind to their own fate. Send a rider to my mother and tell her not to come. She will understand, she will know she can do nothing now."

Nathan pulled the reins of his horse and turned his mount away from the blood-soaked fields before leading his closest advisers away at a gallop. They had much riding to do and many miles to travel before they would reach their destination. And he had much to consider before he could come up with the answers. The sooner he got back to the castle and could converse with his mother he would be able to see things more clearly, her wisdom would be most welcome.

As the prince rode away he did not realise he was being watched. From its lofty perch in one of the trees a bird surveyed the scene. A crow, a carrion bird, but this creature wasn't searching the carnage for its next meal. Instead its gaze followed the prince as he rode off on his white mount. Around its neck the bird wore a bright green jewel in the centre of a black necklace. The stone was not there as a thing of beauty, it had another purpose. None except the person who had placed it around the bird's neck actually knew the purpose of the jewel.

Its purpose was to serve as an eye for the one who had a hold over it. From far off the witch was able to survey the same scene that lay in front of the crow and what she was able to see pleased her greatly. Many men and beasts had died at her bidding but she paid little heed to their lifeless bodies. They mattered nothing to her. What she saw filled her with nothing but happiness. The sight of the prince riding away, a look of pain and anguish on his face, brought a broad smile to her face. In his moment of greatest triumph he had turned tail and left the field of battle and soon he would be spreading the news of her new army sweeping through the land. She had hoped to wait until her main forces could join the battle but the prince's impatience had sought to weaken his own forces and make her victory all the more likely. Like wildfire the news would spread across the land and carry all before it on a tide of fear. With a cackle of satisfaction she turned from the scene in the pool of water upon which she had been gazing into. Things were working out very nicely, she thought to herself. Soon the knight would be dead, along with the Queen and all of her family. She would be able to reign over a land and a people, these miserable people who had shunned her, she had long known it was her right to be the ruler over. A birth right which had been stolen from her and one which she would reclaim. With the help of the dragon and her offspring in keeping that meddlesome knight in check she had been able to put all of her plans into process and very nicely they were all working out.

Chapter 12

Long into the hours of darkness the queen and her son talked of what they must do. What they could do to help the people, to save the land which it was not only their duty but also their honour to serve. Day was breaking when they finally turned with heavy hearts and ordered their people to leave the castle and take to the hills, to seek refuge anywhere they could in a land which was to become overrun by the forces of untold and uncontrollable evil.

"Nathan," said the Queen.

"Yes mother, what is it?" he asked.

"I'm worried for you and your sister. What sort of a land is this for the likes of you to rule over?"

"Don't worry, Livi and I will be fine. After all, she's got Dillon with her and she's a tough little thing as well, don't forget," he replied. "We are your children, you know."

"Yes, you're right," she said, but she could not disguise the trepidation in her voice, her mouth trembling slightly as she tried in vain to keep her emotions in check.

'What is to become of them?' she wondered to herself as they made their way to the courtyard where they mounted the horses which the servants held steady for them.

Three hours later the horses were fit for no more as the Queen and the prince reached their destination. They had ridden through the day to reach the castle at Eloog, a far-off stronghold built into the shadow of a mountain which would be easier to defend than their own home. At least the people would be safe for a time there as Deborah Anne and Nathan pitted their wits to come up with an answer to the problem which now presented itself to them, one which could prove fatal not only for their family and their dynasty but also for their nation.

"What are we to do? It will only be a matter of time before we are overrun and everybody is slain," said the Queen.

"I don't know. We will fight, for what good it will do, and the forces of the witch will bleed heavily before we allow them to breach the castle walls," replied her son.

Getting off their horses they greeted the captain of the guard who was not surprised to see the royal family and their army join him in the home he normally shared with just a handful of men and a few rats. And they had hundreds of ordinary people – scared people – with them. 'Some use they will be when the fighting starts,' the captain thought to himself.

The captain turned on his heels and set about the job of organising his men and a rag-bag group of civilians to the work of shoring up the defences. It was going to take a lot of hard work and maybe some luck too if they were going to be able to repel the forces of evil from their stronghold. By the latest reports, brought to their ears by the scouts who had arrived within the last half hour, the witch's army was only a day's march from them as it swept all before it, cutting and burning a path across the land, leaving a bloody trail in its wake.

The captain turned his gaze to the Stuck Pig, the ale house on the nearest corner. At least some hardy souls were making the most of it, enjoying their time while they still could and fortifying themselves with ale for the battles which lay ahead. Wearily he turned back to his task and busied himself with ordering the strengthening of the defences.

Darkness was falling once again and the men were weary from the long toil which had occupied them through the baking sun of the day.

As the captain took a long drink from his canteen he looked up at the nearest tree to see the crow sat on one of the branches and caught sight of the bright jewel suspended around its neck, shivering as if something evil had cast its gaze upon him. As if to hide the shame he felt at being scared he quickly turned away.

The captain and his tired men, toiling vainly to reinforce the castle walls following years of neglect which had seen them crumble and crack, came into the vision of the witch who allowed herself a cackle of delight.

"Fools, fools, they labour in vain," she said.

"But they can wait. As they busy themselves with their worthless toil I have more important matters to attend to. The knight is mine and soon I will have the meddlesome princess and her dog too. Then I can deal with the Queen and the prince. I have waited long for this moment and soon it will be here. Oh how I am going to enjoy myself at long last as the ruler of this miserable land and its pathetic citizens. How they will grovel as they beg for their lives. Oh what fun it will be to squeeze the life out of every last one of them."

The witch turned away from the pool of water and moved across the inn which was her home for the night. Sending her scouts out to check the land ahead of tomorrow's advance she busied herself formulating the plans in her head. She would give the Queen and the prince the battle they expected but that was just a cover, a smoke screen for her plans. The witch intended to invade the land and quickly take control and then rule with fear. If she could take both the knight and the Queen out of the picture she would take away all hope from the people and they would quickly bow to her will. Many long and bitter years she had lived in the wilderness after being banished from what she regarded was her birth right and now she was back to reclaim it. People would pay for what she had to suffer through during those years and she was determined the pain of her vengeance would long trouble their minds.

Chapter 13

They came as light first broke over the horizon, thousands of wild men and beasts howling and screaming as they spread like fire across the valley which lay before the castle. The witch had committed only a small part of her army but the expendable were more than enough to keep the Queen and the prince occupied while she busied herself with adding the princess to the knight she already had in the bag. Oh what a pretty collection they would make locked up in the deepest dungeons. She would take great pleasure in watching them rot in jail as the spirit slowly leached out of them. All of the pain she had gone through would all seem worthwhile in the anguished expressions of the Queen and her offspring as they had to cope with the torment of the witch ruling these lands.

As the witch's army swept through the valley the men on the castle walls hefted their shields and readied their swords and spears. The bowmen loaded their weapons with arrows and as the captain gave the order they released their deadly projectiles into the advancing army. At the same time the catapults released their cargo of rocks into the swathes of advancing men and beasts. Many men and animals crumbled under the fatal barrage which greeted them, the field quickly turning red as blood was spilled. But with every body that fell ten more were there to take its place. It wasn't long before the witch's forces were swarming over the castle walls as fierce hand-to-hand fighting broke out. Bravely, the Queen's forces repelled every attack and slowly they managed to beat back the forces of evil but they knew what respite they earned was probably only temporary.

During a short lull in the fighting the captain mopped his brow and looked out across the castle walls. The lines were holding but the cost to both sides was a heavy one. All about lay lifeless figures and the foul stench of death filled the air, day turned dark as fires raged and the sun burned down from the sky.

For a brief moment the captain's mind turned to his family. He prayed they had found safety, had somehow found sanctuary in the land where fear reigned. His wife and children had been left behind on the farm he had left to take up arms when the Queen's call had come. At least his home was on the far reaches of the land and well away from the current focus of the witch's forces. He hoped against hope that his beautiful wife and children could somehow be spared the evil and he could be reunited with them.

Just then his attention was taken by a blur just on the edge of his vision. But too late he realised the blur was the shaft of an arrow which buried itself in his chest. Jolted by the force as the serrated tip of the arrow pierced his chest he grasped the shaft and cried out in pain. With a picture of his smiling family the last thing in his mind, he drew his final breath before collapsing to the ground.

Chapter 14

Livi sat with her arms folded and a grim look on her face. She had warned Dillon they were taking the wrong path but he had refused to listen. And that silly dog had led them straight into a trap. Now they were at the bottom of a foul and stinking hole as crows circled overhead, no doubt alerting anyone who cared to listen to their helpless presence at the bottom of the pit.

Dillon and William had spent many minutes wasting their energy trying to climb the sheer sides of their new-found prison. Livi was far too busy for that, busy thinking her way out of this particular little problem. If only they had stayed on the main path instead of forging out into the trees as Dillon had insisted. But enough of how they had got into this predicament, how they were going to get out was all that mattered now. But it wasn't Livi who found the way out as ropes appeared over the sides of the pit.

"Quickly, climb out," called out a young voice.

Needing no second prompt the companions quickly scaled the sides of the pit but as they pulled themselves over the edge they realised they had been tricked. For rather than a friendly face they saw the source of the voice was a dragon, with a much bigger and much uglier dragon stood behind it. Stood all around were a group of heavily armed men and amidst them laughing loudly was the evil lord.

"So, sport it is then for me at last," he said as he let out a loud belly laugh.

Tremgara turned one eye towards the lord and snorted a blast of flame from her nostrils.

"Hold fast. The witch's orders are that these three are to join the knight and await the arrival of the other members of this regal family. Once they are all together and the witch has power over this land then you can enjoy yourself as much as you want. Until then you do as you are told. There will be time enough for enjoyment later."

Bitterly disappointed, the lord snorted as he surveyed their captives.

"Bind them and put them with the knight," said the evil lord.

"They will keep but I will have my sport, of that I promise you by everything I have and all that I hold dear."

Dejectedly the friends were marched away in chains by the men as the dragons flew off in the direction of their lair.

No one noticed the two small girls peering from behind a tree as the men and their captives followed the lord who rode on his horse at the head of the procession.

They had not gone far before the calm of the forest was shattered by a loud bang. A flash of light accompanied the noise as the men all dived for cover.

"Attack, we are under attack," cried the lord. "Fight back, hold fast, don't run," he added.

But before the men realised what was happening their prisoners had been freed and made good their escape, leaving the lord to curse his men into belated action.

"Fools, someone will pay for this," raged the lord. "I am thwarted again."

"And that's not all," cried Tremgara as she and Raygon swooped down upon the scene.

"You've let them escape. The witch will not be best pleased. I rather think you will be the one paying the price of your failure," screamed the older dragon as she drew fire from deep in her belly and blasted it towards the men in jets from both of her nostrils.

The fire engulfed the trees and also claimed several of the men. The lord was badly burned but left alive, Tremgara knowing that the witch would wish to administer her own particular brand of punishment.

The smell of burning flesh and the pained cries of the men filled the air, cries which the fleeing friends could hear all too clearly as they made their way as quickly as their feet would take them.

For many minutes they ran quickly through the woods, following the two sisters who led them this way and that. Eventually they stopped and were able to rest, taking their time to catch their breath.

"That was a close one, thanks to all that is good that you were there to get us out of trouble," said Dillon, his tongue sticking out of his mouth as he panted in an attempt to cool down.

"Yes, lucky for you they were there. Thanks once again for your assistance," said Livi.

"Ok, ok, I admit you were right and I was wrong," added the breathless dog.

Chapter 15

"You need to leave this place, you can't stay, it's too dangerous," said Hattie.

"We know, but where are we to go? We are looking for the knight. Do you know where he is?" asked Livi.

"The dragons have him in their lair. Just to get there will be perilous and will take you a long time unless you know the way. We will show you where to go but we can't help you if helping him to escape is what you are about. We daren't."

"That's ok, we can do that bit, it's just we don't know where we are supposed to go to find the dragons' lair. Once you have shown us the way we will help the knight escape, or at least try to."

"You need to be aware of some of the things which will face you along the way. Do not talk to anyone with one eye, they can't be trusted. And don't accept a lift from anyone with one leg. Or accept food from anyone who has only one hand. Apart from that, you should be safe."

Livi, Dillon and William exchanged glances, all three wondering about people with only one eye, one leg or one hand. Livi shrugged and her companions thought it was better not to ask, for not only did it appear rude but it could easily provide an answer none of them really wanted to hear. As no news was good news at least they wouldn't be carrying the burden in their hearts if they had asked what the girl meant and received an unwelcome answer in return.

Slowly and quietly they followed the sisters as they led the way through the forest. It was getting late and the friends resigned themselves to a long walk in the fading light, each knowing their journey might well have only just started rather than be nearing its conclusion.

As they wended their way along the forest track they were watched by the creatures, birds and squirrels looking over them as they made their weary way. But animals were not the only ones who saw were they were going. For they were followed by a crow, a crow wearing a bright jewel of green about its neck. And that meant one thing. Also watching them was the witch, planning her next move to thwart their quest and at the same time promote her own evil plans.

The witch wasn't on the princess's mind. She could only focus on what drove her forward, her promise to her mother to free the knight and hopefully set off a chain of events which would, in itself, thwart the witch. Only the knight had the power to stop the witch, her mother had told her that. Livi's thoughts turned to her mother, she wondered for the first time in a long time if she was safe and what she was doing.

Chapter 16

Long into the night the Queen and the prince conversed, reading ancient texts and old books as they tried in vain to find an answer to their problem. They had to come up with a way of stopping the witch. Not that they didn't have faith in Livi to rescue the knight, but they were looking for another way, just in case things didn't work out for Livi and also to buy the princess more time. And, of course, in the event the unthinkable happened. What if Livi didn't succeed? What if the dragons had already slain the knight?

But the longer they searched for the answer and the harder they tried the further the truth they sought appeared to be from their grasp. Several times they found a promising clue in the texts of the ancient wizards only for it to come to a dead end. Several times they argued, not bitterly, about what was the solution to their vexed search. Time after time they went back to the beginning and re-read the clues which all started with the riddle.

The riddle had been written by Yror, most ancient and wise of the wizards who came from the Land of Green, where wisdom had long dwelt and where men with long white beards were venerated.

A lover of music, the wise Yror had written many texts but he was most widely celebrated for the ballads he had composed. Many of the books on the shelves of the royal palaces of this land and those about it were full of his texts and songs and his fame had spread far and wide across lands both near and distant.

Once, twice, three times call.
Looking for the answer.
Under the stone you will find it.

Somewhere close to the heartbeat.

"Oh, what's the answer?" asked the Queen, as much in desperation as anything else. She thought about giving up the search many times over that night but again she found herself making a fresh start, drawing from the prince the strength to carry on in the same way he was inspired not to give up.

A knock came at the door to the room where they sat, a roaring fire keeping the chill from their bones. Faintly in the distance they could hear the sounds of fighting – men screaming and shouting, boulders smashing and burning wood cracking – and it got louder as the door opened.

"Sire, My Lady, I have news," said the messenger as he entered the room.

"How goes the battle?" asked the prince.

"Well, we repel every attack. But there is a feeling amongst the captains that they do not commit their full force. That they hold something in reserve and can, at any time, hit the walls with such force that they would just crumble like sticks and we would be overrun."

"We need to make arrangements in case that happens, Nathan, we need to be ready to get the women and children to safety."

"What would you suggest, Mother?" asked the prince, fearful men at arms would be taken from the task in hand in order to prepare an evacuation. The prince had no desire to turn tail and run, he was focused on fighting off the enemy and turning the evil tide from this land once and for all. His birth right was at stake and, like any prince worth the name, he would not bow down to a witch.

Something came to the Queen and she was drawn away from her son's gaze. He stared at her and was angry at her failure to answer, the impetuous element to his character urging him to rebuke the Queen; he had little time for this fruitless search for an answer to the riddle and even less time to sit there and be ignored.

"Well, I'm waiting for an answer," he demanded. "What do you suggest we do about getting the women and children out of here? Still, if we lose the battle they may as well be dead anyway. So I don't see much point in planning an evacuation."

"Quiet, I'm thinking," replied the Queen as she raised a hand to emphasise her desire not to be disturbed as the answer suddenly came to her.

"That's it. The riddle," she exclaimed. "The answer's been there all the time but we were too blind to see."

Slowly the Queen lifted her hands to the three-jewelled pendant she wore on the end of a gold chain around her neck.

The Stones of the Green Land, three emeralds which shone brightly. As she turned the pendant over in her hands she repeated the riddle aloud.

"Once, twice, three times call. Looking for the answer. Under the stone you will find it. Somewhere close to the heartbeat.

"All this time and it was around my neck, three stones, worn close to my heartbeat. Yror knew what he was doing when he gave me this, it was just a pity I couldn't see what he meant until now."

The Queen looked around the room until her gaze fell on what she sought, a wooden club. She walked over and hefted the club in her fist, placing the pendant down on a stone table and swinging the club high above her left shoulder and brought it crashing down on to the biggest of the three stones, the third stone as it was known. As the emerald shattered it revealed a golden coin which had been hidden inside. The coin made a ringing sound as it span to a halt on the table. The Queen picked the coin up in her left hand and held it up in the faint light so she could see what was written on it.

"The child that whistles can calm the evil." That was the text upon the coin.

"The child that whistles can calm the evil," the Queen said aloud. "What does that mean?"

"Whistling, I hate whistling. The princess does it all the time when she's playing with that dumb dog," said the prince.

"That's it… whistling," said the Queen. "Livi whistles, the child that whistles. Oh my daughter's the answer."

But as it came to her the answer filled the Queen with dread. She had sent her daughter off to rescue a knight when that task of great importance had been overtaken by one of even higher significance.

Chapter 17

The witch sat in her favourite chair. Not that she had many favourites, things that she liked or cared about. Love was out of the question because it was something she could not feel. Some had accused her of only loving herself but she was not sure that even that was true.

As she sat there she stroked her familiar and the animal, her closest companion yet not her friend, purred loudly as it hoped desperately for the affection that was so rarely shown to continue. However, the cat was, like its mistress, a creature more predisposed to cruelty rather than affection. For many hours of the day it spent its time either watching the crow or thinking up ways to kill it. Eating the bird was out of the question because of its size but the cat definitely wanted to kill it. It probably tasted foul anyway. But the desire to kill the bird which mocked it with every look would not be easy. The bird was high in the esteem of Malfer's mistress and the plan would have to be cunning to succeed.

"No Malfer, stop those thoughts," said the witch in a barely audible voice which carried more menace than a dragon's breath or the beady look of the malign crow.

"I know what you desire. But kill that bird and I will crush you until you are just so much dust in my hand. The crow has a purpose far above any you could fulfil for me and one for which I can forgive it any crime and so I place it above all others in my thoughts."

The cat sighed and leapt from her lap, consoling itself with the thought that despite her ability to read its mind, that the day would one day come when the roles would be reversed.

With the cat having taken its unwelcome desires off to a far corner of the room the witch turned her thoughts to the one part of her plan which could yet prove to be her downfall.

The princess was occupied with the knight and as long as the dragons were able to delay her return to the Queen then there would be enough time for the plan to succeed. As the witch sat there and considered her plans she smiled to herself at the irony of the situation.

"Yes, little do they know that they have the power to defeat me," she said aloud.

"And in one so sweet and innocent, it is ironic that they think the most important task is to rescue the knight. Drawing their prize asset away from the real task was a masterstroke of mine. As long as the princess is occupied with the knight they have lost the power to stop me."

Little did the witch know her words were not a private conversation with herself; an airing of the deep thoughts which grew in her mind, but which ultimately came from her blackened heart which needed as much to suck the life out of other beings to exist as it did to draw breath.

Unknown to the witch she was being watched. From her hiding place in the corner of the room Millie watched and listened with intent. But listening and knowing what to do with the information were two completely different things and the question of what to do vexed the little girl. Also on her mind was what she had done, putting herself at risk to visit the lair of the witch. Hattie would be beside herself with worry if she knew what her sister had been doing. After giving the whole question much thought Millie decided she would have to tell Hattie. Although she did not know what she could do with the information she knew it was important enough to ask her sister what should be done.

Getting away from the witch was easy enough but finding her sister was going to be the difficult bit. Millie knew Hattie was probably in The Hiding Tree but getting there was another matter. Many miles lay between where she was and where she wanted to be and Millie feared capture by the forces of evil which she knew would lie in her path.

The little girl slipped quickly from her hiding place as the witch slept and soon she was journeying through the forest.

Millie had travelled many miles, more than she cared to calculate, when she finally found herself a place to sleep as she collapsed into a deep slumber in the hollow of a tree, a place she hoped would be safe. But she was mistaken.

"Well my lovely, what are you doing here then?" said a gruff voice as a calloused hand reached out and grabbed Millie by the neck.

She was woken roughly from her sleep and found herself being dangled by one ankle by a big, fat, ugly man. As she struggled as violently as she could, the little girl could see her captor, all anger and with a face that had seen many years of bad experiences and very little love. She feared not only for her freedom but also for her life. Any thoughts of the witch, the princess, the knight and least of all the safety of the kingdom were pushed well to the deepest recesses of her mind.

Millie suffered an uncomfortable journey, trussed up with her hands bound to her ankles and thrown into a sack. She had managed to hear snatches of conversation as she was carried along, suspended in the sack from a pole. All she had been able to make out were the humdrum parts of everyday life which her captor and his companions had talked about, passing time as they trudged wearily to their destination.

Millie landed with a thud on the cold stone floor and took a few brief moments composing herself before she was able to get her bearings.

"Right, what shall we do with you, I wonder?" asked the same man who had captured her.

"We could kill her, but I doubt the lord would want that," replied another man as five figures crowded over her, their large shapes becoming more distinct as Millie's eyes became more accustomed to the halflight which the torches, burning with an acrid smell, threw across the room which was now her prison.

"He will want her for himself, so he can decide how she dies. He might be prepared to pay for her, or we could ransom her to her family, if she has some," added the same man.

"Let's find out who she is and where she's from," said a third, the wicked grin on his face giving more than a hint towards the methods he aimed to employ in his pursuit of that knowledge.

Millie gulped in a big breath of air and knew there was only one way she could escape because time was a commodity she had little of in the bank. During the journey she had come to realise she must escape as quickly as possible. She had to find the princess, or the Queen, or anybody who could help thwart the witch's evil plans.

As the men crept forward a flash of blinding light pierced the darkness and left them staggering around, sweeping out with their arms as they tried to come to terms with what had happened.

What she had done was use a magic spell she had been given by a friendly wizard. Millie carried the spells wrapped in special paper in a purse attached to her belt. All she had to do was take one out and throw it to the floor and the blinding light it gave off caused enough confusion for her to escape. She also had the secret incantation, the words she had to say each time she used the spell to stop it having the same effect upon her or those she sought to help.

Those moments of confusion were all that Millie needed, the girl running freely through the open cell door which the men had carelessly, but conveniently for her, left ajar. As she raced up the never-ending stairs she started to feel a fresh breeze on her face which was a more than welcome relief after breathing in the foul stench of death which was so strong it almost seemed to work its way into the pores of everyone who was exposed to it. She was not sad that her time in that place had been but brief.

The men came to their senses but it was too late.

"What do we do now, he will be mad?" said one.

"Not if we don't tell him. Come, place your right hands on mine and swear an oath that not one of us shall breathe a word of this and not one shall hear of what has gone on here."

As he finished the sentence the other four men each placed a right hand, one on top of the other, in an act of bonding which meant they were tied together for the rest of their days. They repeated the same oath, which they knew if broken would force the other four to kill he who had broken it, three times.

"None shall know," they said as one.

Millie was relieved to be free of her captors. She was running as quickly as she could go and, as anyone who knew her knew, that was far faster than any human and not far slower than the swiftest horse. But she still had a long way to go and not much idea of where she was going. She had decided she must go home, to The Hiding Tree, but was not sure that was the right place to go. If for no other reason than she knew she would feel safe when she got there she decided to trust her instincts.

She had not bargained on being followed but she was. The crow was tracking her escape, following her rapid path with ease. The crow knew its purpose and it enjoyed being the eyes of the witch. True, it thought to itself as it tracked the girl, there were times when the evil intentions the cat had towards it made it doubt its safety but as long as it remained in the favour of the witch it knew safety was guaranteed. Or so it thought, perhaps mistakenly so.

For many hours they travelled in unison, the girl running like the wind and the bird following, undetected by its prey.

Millie knew she was tiring and she also knew she had been followed for some time by the bird. She had been careful not to let on she knew and hoped her plan to lose her pursuer would be successful. If she could reach the crofter's cottage on the edge of the wood she was certain she would be able to get away. An hour later she saw the cottage come into view and checked, carefully, that the bird was still following her. When she was satisfied the bird was still there Millie slowed her run to a walk and prepared herself for the next part of her plan.

Once inside the cottage she removed her hat and cloak and arranged them, with the use of a chair and a broom, to make it look as if she was sitting at a table with her back to the window.

About a hundred paces from the cottage the crow perched on the branch of an ancient oak. For several minutes it sat there before the jewel about its neck began to glow.

Far away, the witch was able to see the same scene as the crow. She did not know the full meaning of what she was seeing but realised there was some significance to the scene, some important message the crow was trying to relay to her. Without delay she summoned one of her most trusted captains and had him take a party of men, about twenty in all and all on horseback, to the cottage. The witch felt good, pleased she was getting closer to her evil desires, confident her plan was working.

What she did not know was that the little girl she had a mind to capture had once again evaded her pursuers. Millie had entered the tunnel, the tunnel Hattie had shown her, through a hatch under the bed in the back room of the cottage. She was long gone by the time the captain and his men arrived at the cottage. Luckily for the crow it was out of their reach when the men discovered they had been duped. After studying the scene for a few moments they had decided the girl was alone. They crept stealthily up to the cottage before, when the captain gave the signal, they burst through the front door. As he reached out to grab the girl the first man realised what was afoot. He let out an anguished cry and began searching the rest of the room. Luckily for Millie her deception had bought her enough time and she was long gone by the time the trap door was discovered.

The captain dispatched two of his smallest men down the tunnel for it was a confined space and only really suitable for use by the dwarves who had built it or by small children like Millie.

The captain then wondered how he was going to tell the witch. He also wondered if he could get away with blaming the crow but the bird had already decided the safest course of action was to be as far away from there and as quickly as possible. Dealing with the witch's wrath was something he could thankfully put off for a long time, a very long time if he could help it.

Chapter 18

Dillon watched over the princess as she slept fitfully. He knew she was fighting some kind of demons in her mind and that she was in peril. But he also knew he could not help her, dare not wake her as this was a battle she had to win on her own.

Livi stopped for a moment, taking care to look around and get her bearings, to discover where she was.

Looking down she saw that her skin was covered in grey fur and where her arms should be there were legs, where her hands and fingers should be were paws and claws. She sniffed the air, pointing her long snout upwards to get a taste of the scents. Nervously she rubbed her nose with her front paws and rubbed her whiskers and eyes.

A new smell came to her senses, jerking her consciousness into life and the mouse looked nervously around her, pushing her head to one side to concentrate her hearing.

"Now, where are you?" she asked herself. "I know you are here and as long as I can avoid you and your evil intentions, the battle, for the time being, will be won."

Livi froze as she heard the faintest of footfalls. There was no mistaking it, that was the sound of a cat pacing through the house. Livi knew from the direction the sound was emanating that she could not directly escape. She would have to use her wits to survive.

"Oh princess. Where are you?" enquired the cat. Or rather the witch. For it was the form of one of her familiars which the witch had chosen for this particular face-off.

Livi shivered uncontrollably. It took several seconds for her to regain control of herself, regulating her skittering heartbeat and trying with all her will to formulate her ideas in some sort of sense so she could work her way out of this trap. She knew it had been a massive risk, with possibly fatal consequences, to seek out confrontation with the witch. Doing it this way meant no other person was put at risk. However, apart from putting her chosen alter ego of the mouse at risk there was the danger its death could leave her trapped inside her own mind, never able to regain consciousness in the real world. Lost forever to those she loved, her mother and her brother and father and the dog that was her constant companion. It was a fight she dare not lose. But it was also a fight that gave to the winner a major advantage. She might not be able to trap the witch in the cat's body and that, honestly, was not the purpose she had in mind. Winning this way could rob the witch of much of her power as she would need great strength and resolve to return to the real world. That would leave the princess with the upper hand in the battle to come, the battle for the Land of The Hiding Tree.

The witch purred contentedly to herself, the sound reverberating around her throat as she stalked from one room to the next.

Livi scanned the room, shifting her gaze quickly from one item of furniture to the next. There was a chance but she would be throwing caution to the wind. She backed herself against any adversary even if this one was the most feared of all. She waited patiently until she heard the cat get closer, looking often over her shoulder to the direction from which she knew it was approaching.

The cat stalked slowly, then it bent down on its front paws and was ready to pounce on the mouse. As it shifted on all four paws and leapt forward the mouse was already affecting its escape. The cat landed with a crash, its mind filled with the disappointment of having missed out on its prey. As it skidded across the polished floor the cat fixed its focus on the rear end of the mouse as it disappeared behind the dresser against the far wall.

'Good, I have the princess trapped. Now for the kill. I will enjoy this,' thought the witch.

She stood still for several seconds, repeating the spell in her mind before saying it aloud. Anyone listening would have only heard a purr and would need to be a cat to understand the incantation.

"Locked away, no escape for you, sweet princess," was the final line. Secure in the knowledge she had blocked off one end of the dresser, the cat walked to the other.

Livi was scared, her whiskers twitching and her nose sniffing the air, but she was determined not to give away that she knew what the witch plotted.

The cat sat around the corner of the dresser and waited. Folding its front paws in front of it as it ran through its mind the fun it was going to have tormenting the mouse before killing it.

The witch was not disturbed when she heard the mouse squeak as the fear took over its prey.

Several minutes passed by before the cat became impatient and peered around the corner. What she saw filled her with anger and she shrieked loudly. At the other end of the dresser was the skin of the mouse. She had been tricked. Before she could move, let alone change back into the witch she was grabbed from behind by two powerful hands.

The princess chanted her own spell.

"Stay in form," she repeated over and over.

The cat struck out with its front claws and kicked with its back legs. Tightly the princess held on, shifting her left hand to grab the animal around the scruff of the neck.

Livi held on tight until the cat stopped struggling and no sounds came from its mouth. The princess knew she could not kill the cat as the witch's inner strength would be too strong for her, even if it had been weakened by casting the spell to seal off one end of the dresser.

Instead the princess would have to trap the animal. That would give her time to get away and also drain much of the witch's power in escaping. She would eventually escape but Livi would be long gone and the witch would be weakened for the battles to come.

Livi called out another spell and opened the door to the dresser before throwing the cat inside. With the animal temporarily incapacitated by the spell Livi quickly cast another.

"Seal the cell," she cried out. She waited for sounds from inside as the cat stirred. She could hear the cat scratch at the door then loud banging as it threw itself at the inside of the door, the accompanying wailing and spitting filling the room with a cacophony of noises.

Her work done Livi exited the room through the portal which she had drawn open with another spell.

Livi awoke to see Dillon staring into her eyes.

"Is it done?" he asked.

"Yes it is. The witch's ego was her undoing. I thank you for the idea. Now we have other work to do."

Chapter 19

Smy paced up and down impatiently. He did not like to be kept waiting, there was nothing he hated more than being kept waiting. But he also knew he could do nothing about it. He knew his place in the greater order of things and he knew it would do him nothing but harm to complain about it to the Great Wizard.

Smy came from the Land of Thers and had been in the service of the wizard, or the Great Wizard as he knew him, for longer than he cared to remember. It was not that he enjoyed what he did but more that he felt it was the work he had been destined to carry out. And besides, any thought of escaping the service of the wizard filled him with dread because of the evil consequences his master would bring down upon him if he tried.

From the next room the wizard could hear Smy pacing up and down and, in his evil mind, it pleased him to keep the snivelling servant waiting. Smy was there at his beck and call, there to carry out his dirty work, to be his bagman. It would do Smy good to wait on someone else instead of being the one keeping people waiting. When the wizard had some dirty job he wanted doing, when he needed someone taking out of the way and dealing with, it was Smy he always turned to. Smy was very resourceful, well versed in the dark arts and the secretive way of getting difficult things done with the minimum of fuss and effort.

Finally the wizard clicked his fingers and Smy came immediately through the door which had opened at the command of the wizard. Smy stood in front of his master with his hands clasped behind his back.

"How goes the work of the witch?" asked the wizard.

"Presently not that well," came Smy's curt reply.

"What? Why? What is that fool playing it?" demanded the wizard, his booming voice full of anger and spite.

"She has been trapped by the princess and will need your help if she is to escape."

"Has she, indeed. Well let her be for a while. I will release her when we have need of her again. If those dragons do their job we won't need her again and she can be left to rot. What of the meddlesome children?"

"I have three of them safe, the sisters and the young boy. I can deal with the princess as well in the same way if you like."

The wizard thought for some time before waving his left hand nonchalantly.

"Whatever you think best. Be gone and deal with this mess. And don't bother me again until everything is in place. We will let the witch take the kingdom for her own but make sure she knows who is really the master here, who rules all dominions and the peasants that dwell within. Now, go, I am sick of the sight of you, Bagman."

Smy lifted the leather briefcase which he had placed by his side when he entered. Bagman was the nickname given to him by the people of the kingdom and the other lands thereabouts. It was because he was the wizard's servant, the one who carried his bag and did his bidding. When there was a particularly unsavoury task needed carrying out the wizard would call on Bagman who would dispatch the duty with clinical and uncaring efficiency.

Smy walked down the draughty corridors of the wizard's place and out into the courtyard. He climbed the steps which had been placed next to the dragon as it slept in the courtyard.

"Come, Mallov, transport me away," demanded Smy.

The dragon opened one eye and snorted loudly, flame firing out of his nostrils and scorching the earth black.

In one swift movement the creature was up on its four legs. A quick beat of its wings lifted Mallov and his passenger clear of the ground and he flew off quickly into the distance.

From his hiding place, Prince Nathan watched as the dragon swooped overhead. When it was clear into the distance the prince mounted his horse and gave orders to the next rider.

"Return to the Queen and tell her Smy of Thers is in pursuit of the princess. Tell her he already has the sisters and the young boy. Also tell her I have not, as yet, found my sister but that I will continue looking. If the princess is to evade capture and fulfil the story of the riddle we need to keep her out of Smy's briefcase. Only then can we defeat the witch. But also warn her that defeating the witch is no longer enough. We also have to beat the wizard, and that's a whole different thing to do."

The messenger rode off and Nathan sat for many minutes, clearing his head of many things and trying to decide which direction he needed to take. He had put off looking in the Dragon Land until the very last but it was something which he could avoid no longer.

From his saddle on the back of Mallov, Smy surveyed the mountainous land which separated the wizard's domain from the kingdom. He reached out and picked up his briefcase from where he had placed it. He undid the two metal clasps and opened the case, laying it flat across the dragon's scaly back. Smy smiled to himself as he looked at the three miniature figures strapped securely into the leather bindings of the case. Each was an exact representation of a real person. Or so it appeared. On closer inspection the figurines appeared lifelike. For they were. Millie and Hattie, and William, were all three trapped there. If it were not for the physical features being exactly the same as the three children you would not have known it were them. They were all in a very deep sleep, albeit with their eyes wide open, and their limp bodies gave away little of the fact that their minds were still active. All three had been trapped by Smy who had used the powers given to him by the wizard to put them in a state of paralyses and shrink them in size until they could fit easily into his bag. After several moments of reflection, during which he fantasised about what he would do to them if the wizard allowed it, Smy closed the case back up and secured the fastenings before making sure it was secure between the two ridges which edged the dragon's back and also served as the mountings for the saddle.

Smy knew it would not be as easy to capture the princess who, after all, had outwitted the witch. But if he could capture the young girl the rewards he would receive would be great, and none greater than the gratitude of his master. That was the one thing he craved more in the world, except save for taking his master's place but that was one dream he only rarely dared to allow himself to have.

He also had another desire and that was to rule the kingdom. He wanted to rub out the Queen and her children and then sit upon the royal throne. He wanted more than anything to be a king. He desired the wealth it would bring and also to have servants to be at his beck and call in the same way he was forced to work for the wizard.

Chapter 20

Nathan rode for many days, or so it seemed, but always he knew he was losing ground on Smy. He never really got close enough to the wizard's deed-doer but had quickly decided the best way to find his sister was to follow Smy who had an uncanny knack of knowing where to find people or creatures.

Nathan was about to give up his pursuit when he came across another traveller, an old man dressed in rags and bent almost double standing by the side of the forest track. The man looked infirm, holding himself up on a long stick which he held in his left hand. Nathan was sure he had some food in his horse's saddle bags which he could spare for the old man. He dismounted and was about to turn and reach into the bag for the food when there was a strange sound, almost like moaning, which emanated from the man's mouth. A blinding flash and a searing pain in his head were the last things Nathan remembered.

When he became aware of where he was again he knew what had happened. The old man had been Smy and he had set a trap which Prince Nathan had fallen into. He was now bound alongside the sisters and another boy and was unable to move a muscle. He was aware of where he was but the only thing he was able to work was his mind and it had gone into overdrive.

He had allowed himself to be trapped and left his sister at the mercy of Smy and who knows what else. He had failed to warn Livi of the dangers she faced and also could do nothing to stop the advance of the evil forces. He now relied on Livi, or someone else, to get him out of this predicament, in time to be of use to his mother in the battle to save the kingdom. If they could not get to Livi and tell her of the need for her to use her special powers everything would be lost. He cursed himself several times before realising that the damage had been done and he was only wasting energy. He needed to try to sleep so he would be rested when the chance to escape presented itself or he was rescued.

As Nathan willed for the relief from his torment which sleep would bring the old man walked along the path, chuckling to himself. He approached a large rock, or what appeared to be a rock, and called out.

"Wake up," he said.

The rock moved and revealed itself to be his dragon.

"Is it done?" asked the dragon, lazily opening one eye and looking unhappy at being disturbed from a deep sleep.

"Yes, I now have the prince to join my little collection of the Sisters of Solace and the boy. All I need now is to capture the princess and I could even go for the full set and take the Queen as well, if the wizard allows it."

Smy looked the dragon in the eye and then pointed a hand to where Nathan's horse was tethered, straining at its leash in a bid to escape the cruel gaze of the winged creature which was looking it up and down and drooling.

"If you're hungry you might as well put that horse to good use, the prince won't be needing it any longer. Do as you are told and you might even get to feed on what I'm carrying in this briefcase."

"That would be very nice. But, in the meantime, horse will do. I am very grateful you have supplied me with such a tasty meal. Thanks you, Smy."

The dragon, which was a much faster animal in the air than on the ground, walked slowly over to the horse as Smy opened his briefcase for another long, lingering look at his captives.

Chapter 21

Livi and Dillon trudged wearily on. They had walked for many miles since they had parted ways with their companions, urging Hattie and William to seek shelter while they went in search of the knight.

Little did the girl or her faithful companion know of what had become of Hattie and William, or Millie and even Nathan for that matter.

"I think we should stop, I'm very hot and very tired. What do you think?" Livi asked the dog.

"As you wish, but we must find cover. I don't like stopping in the open during the day. You never can be too careful of who or what is watching in lands such as these," replied Dillon.

"Some food wouldn't go amiss either, a nice bone to chew on and a long nap would be just right about now."

"Sorry. We've only got biscuits and there aren't many of them left. If you want anything else you will have to find it. And there's not much water left either," added the girl as she lifted her satchel over her head and opened it to examine the contents.

Dillon wasn't paying attention. He had started to walk away with his nose pointed high in the air, sniffing loudly. The dog stopped and his long pink tongue poked out of his mouth and he licked his face with a loud slurp.

"What is it Dillon?" asked Livi.

The dog was still paying her no attention and that was beginning to annoy Livi quite visibly. She was getting quite agitated and was just about to voice her frustration with the dog when what he stopped her just as the words were forming on her lips.

"I can smell sausages," uttered the dog almost in a whisper. I can smell sausages and what's more is it's coming from just over there. Come on, let's see if there's a sausage for us," said Dillon.

"Wait, it could be a trap," exclaimed Livi.

But her words were of no effect. The dog had already disappeared into a thicket of dense green bushes. Livi resigned herself to following the dog and also disappeared through the bushes.

What she found when she appeared on the other side startled her. It was as if she and Dillon had been transported into a different world. Before her she could see a clearing with a bubbling stream and a picturesque cottage. Smoke drifted from the chimney and the air was filled with the delightful smell of cooking sausages, accompanied by the comforting sound of a sizzling frying pan.

As Livi and Dillon stood there nervously the door to the cottage opened slowly and an old woman walked out, taking time and care to measure her small footsteps as she looked long and hard at the girl and the dog stood in front of her.

Eventually the old woman spoke. She said one word.

"Hello."

Then she waited for a reply. Livi was the first to remember her manners.

"Hello. Say hello, Dillon," she added, kicking the dog softly to prompt him into addressing the woman.

"Hello," the dog said, placing his face on his front paws as he lay obediently at Livi's feet.

"You must be Livi and Dillon," said the woman.

"How do you know that?" demanded Livi precociously, a puzzled look on her inquisitive face.

"Oh, I know many things. Some things I should know, some things perhaps I should not know. But nevertheless I know who you are and why you are here. But first let's get to the reason you find yourselves in front of me, you are hungry and have smelt what I am cooking. Please join me for some breakfast and we will talk later."

Chapter 22

Smy enjoyed his work. It was very specialised work but it was work that he did well.

He had been very busy and he was sure the wizard was pleased with what he had achieved. Although he never said so the rejection and lack of love shown to him by the wizard hurt Smy deeply. The pain he felt was deeper than any joy he could feel at having completed his work so efficiently and successfully.

He had spent many months over his task, long in the planning and also long in the execution. But he knew all of his hard work had been worthwhile.

He had collected numerous children and they were all safely stored inside the leather briefcase which he carried everywhere with him, hanging limply from his feeble wrist. However, his body might appear feeble but his mind was not and it was a more powerful weapon to him than any sword or spear a much larger man could yield, even the Fighting Giants of the North who were prepared to sell their fighting skills to the highest bidder.

Smy remembered the Fighting Giants from his time as a child. They scared him then, but not now. Many times they had suffered when they had offended the wizard so they knew not to anger Smy whom they knew to be a close confidant of the wizard. To anger Smy was a certain way to ensure the retribution of the wizard would follow soon afterwards.

Smy's most pleasing capture to date had been the sisters. He had caught the older one, Hattie along with William and had also tracked the younger one, Millie, from when she had escaped from the evil lord. Capturing that one had been particularly pleasing because he had succeeded where the evil lord had failed, and also where the witch had been unaware the girl had watched her. He had now taken the prince as well and he was by far the most prized capture he had taken so far.

Now all that remained was the meddlesome princess. If he could capture that one he would surely be in the favour of the wizard; he would surely love Smy and show everyone that he was his favourite.

Smy smiled as he walked along, formulating a plan in his brain, fitting all of the pieces together in his mind like a child puts together the pieces of a jigsaw.

Chapter 23

Livi and Dillon were both glad to sit and eat and drink. And they ate and drank plenty at the old lady's table. There was bread and meat, cheese and fruit, biscuits and lots of juice to drink.

When they had finished and the old lady busied herself clearing the plates and dishes Livi looked around the sparse cottage from her seat at the table. The walls were not painted and there were no pictures but the cottage had a warm and homely feeling.

"What would you like to ask me?" asked the woman.

"How do you know I want to ask anything?" replied the precocious child.

"Because it's in your nature, I sense it," said the woman.

"But it would be rude for me to ask."

"I don't really think that will be enough to stop you, will it now."

Livi thought for several moments, casting a quick glance at Dillon whose relaxed smile convinced her it was safe to ask questions.

"What is your name?"

"My name is Rose, although I would have thought a more taxing question would have been your first. Now, Livi, is there anything else? Perhaps Dillon would like to ask a question. Your talking dog might come up with something more original."

"You know our names. How?" demanded Livi.

"Oh, I know a great many things about a great many things. Some of them good, some of them bad. But know one thing. I will help you if I can. I don't like the witch, or the wizard, so to help you and your brother and the Queen rid this land of them and their evil servants is something I desire greatly. Especially Smy, that is one particularly nasty individual I would be most glad to see the back of."

"Who's Smy?" asked Livi.

"Someone you have not had the misfortune yet to meet. If you had you might not be here with me now. He's evil but also very crafty and one of the few creatures even you, with your special gifts, needs to be very wary of."

Livi thought a little more and also looked at Dillon as if searching for inspiration over what to do next.

"Look. It is late and the forest is not the nicest place to be at night. If you like you can sleep here with me and then continue your journey in the morning."

Livi was about to ask Dillon what he thought of the suggestion but his snores – he had already fallen asleep – were answer enough.

"I think Dillon has already decided you are staying the night," said Rose.

"Come with me and I will make up a bed for you. Dillon can stay there and guard the door, although the creatures of the forest that are my friends will keep watch."

Nobody knew who the old woman was and Livi had certainly never heard of her before she came upon her. The little girl thought deeply before sleep took her, searching her memory for a clue about the old woman's existence. But she was not alone in her ignorance. Anyone who came across the kind old woman was never able to remember the way back to where they had seen her. As if by magic, the woman was kept safe from the world at large and she revealed herself only to those she trusted. Livi did not encounter the woman again, at least not for a very long time, despite spending many days in the future trying to rediscover her location.

Chapter 24

Nathan dismounted his horse and gritted his teeth as he faced his assailants. They had followed him for more than a day, tracking him as he travelled at speed through broken country.

He knew he had been lucky to escape the one called Smy but had taken a great risk by allowing himself to be captured and imprisoned in the case. Only after pretending to be captured like the rest had he been able to make his escape. He had used an old spell his godmother had taught him and was able to return himself to his normal size. He had thought more than once about freeing the others but hoped they would not mind him making sure his sister was able to carry out her duty, a task upon which the fate of the kingdom now lay.

But there was enough time to think of that later as he turned his mind to the immediate danger which blocked the path ahead of him.

He knew he was getting close to where his sister was; if he could help her free the knight and then return with all haste to their mother they might just be able to save the kingdom. It was, he knew, his sworn duty to try or die in the doing of the task.

The prince held his sword in his right hand and a long-handled dagger in the left. He had decided to stand and fight rather than continue to try his futile bid to lose his pursuers. But foremost in his mind was his desire to deal with these men before he found his sister because he could not allow the princess to be put in danger: her safety and that of the kingdom were now inexorably linked.

What faced Nathan on that wooded path filled his stomach with a tight feeling and made the hairs stand up on the back of his neck. He was not afraid but he was aware of the odds which were stacked heavily against him.

Six men faced him, all battle-hardened veterans long skilled in the craft of war and the grim business of death. Nathan worked out his best option for several long moments before deciding on his best course of action and launching himself at the nearest assailant with a blood-curdling scream and a fleet of hand movement which brought the sword down in an arc on the man's arm. The move was one Nathan had practised many times and it showed in the result, the man's hand being cleaved from his arm and dropping to the ground.

In a state of utter shock, the man looked at his fallen hand before gripping his arm with his other hand and looking around in bewilderment at his companions. As if awakened from sleep the man came to realise what had happened and let out a terrible scream, running off into the forest with blood pumping from a wound which would in several long and painful hours prove fatal.

Nathan launched his attack again, this time clashing swords with the biggest and meanest looking of the men. They were all dark of complexion and, he guessed, mercenaries from the southern lands who had taken the wizard's money and brought fear and destruction to his mother's realm.

Nathan and the man locked swords and came together so they could look each other in the eye from a distance of inches. As they struggled to win this battle of wills and strength the remaining four men formed a circle around them, waiting for a moment to pounce on the smallest opening to strike the prince what they hoped would be a wounding or even a fatal blow.

The fight lasted several minutes and both men were covered in sweat as the noon sun bathed the path in brilliant light.

Nathan had been schooled well in swordsmanship but found his attacker an even match. It would take something special to win this fight.

The man, called by his friends Zeke but named at birth Ezekiel, was beginning to tire of the exertions when he sensed an opening. The prince was a fair swordsman but he had left an opening, one Zeke had seen several times and finally he decided to strike. As Nathan drew back his arm he left his chest exposed and Zeke lunged with his own sword. But what he did not know was that Nathan had been waiting for him to be drawn in. With a quick feint Nathan deflected the blow with his own sword and made his own move with the dagger which he plunged into the man's heart. Zeke spent several seconds motionless as if suspended in air. Finally he let out an anguished sound, something like a frog croaking, before falling face first to the ground.

The other men were shocked by what they saw. They had expected Zeke to win the fight and did not know how to react. Nathan turned quickly this way and that, facing his attackers and swinging his sword before him as if to invite them to challenge him. But they thought better of it, instead deciding to turn on their heels and run.

A relieved Nathan, his energy all but spent, collapsed to his knees and remained there until he had stopped gasping for breath and his heart had slowed from its exaggerated pace.

The prince finally rose to his feet and walked to his horse. Wearily he climbed on the steed and set off in search of Livi.

Chapter 25

Yksboor stirred, not for the first time, from a deep and debilitating sleep. The knight felt something was still very wrong, a weariness in his bones and a fog to his mind which he could not shake off no matter how hard he tried.

Slowly he raised himself to his feet and stood for several minutes as he tried to focus his brain. He had no idea how long he had been there or what had happened while he lay at the mercy of the dragons. Only one thought kept coming back to him, the fact that he must try to get away and back to fulfil his duty to the people.

Slowly he managed to focus his mind and was able to make out something which had bothered him for some time, for a time before he was awake. There was a voice calling him, someone, somewhere, calling his name. It sounded like a very young child, a male child, calling to him. For some reason a name came into his head. The name Charlie was embedded somewhere in his mind, perhaps subconsciously urging him to finally break free of his captors.

Yksboor looked around for a weapon and could see no sword or dagger close to hand. A further examination of the floor of the cave which also served as his dungeon revealed nothing more than a few rocks and some branches. So rather than fight his way out, which was what he knew as he was a knight, he would have to use his mind to engineer an escape.

As Yksboor sat on a rock on the floor of the cave he struggled for what seemed an eternity with his predicament. 'How will I ever escape here?' he asked himself.

It was then he turned his head, straining to hear the noise which was coming from the mouth of the cave. He lifted himself to his feet and walked to the light to find out what was making the noise which, if he was not mistaken, sounded like the song of a bird. He had heard something like it many times when he was a child but it was a sound now very rare in this country because the influence of evil had driven anything with love in its heart to the very extremes of the land.

Yksboor spotted the pretty blue bird perched on a tree branch close to the entrance to the cave.

"What's your purpose being here, I wonder?" Yksboor asked himself as much as to the bird.

"I'm here to help you. My name is Charlie and I am the animal form of your niece's boy child. I am pure of heart and that means the evil forces can't hurt me or taint my mission which is to help you fight to win the freedom of the people of this land."

Yksboor was stunned by what the bird said but soon recovered his wits and accepted what he was told. He had lived too long in this magical land not to believe that humans and animals, both good and evil, could take many forms.

Carefully he measured his words, not wanting to fall into another trap which could have been laid by the dragons and their cohorts.

"So what should we do?" asked the knight.

"That is your choice. I cannot lead you or make your choices but I can give my help if you ask for it," replied the bird.

"Right. I request your help. We need to get away from here. Is there anything you can do which will help me?"

"I think so, wait there," said the bird before flapping its pretty red-tipped wings and flying out of sight.

Yksboor watched as the bird flew away and hoped his own chances of escape were not disappearing.

Shortly the bird returned to its perch.

"I'm sorry to sound impatient, for I know you are here to help, but what have you discovered?" asked the knight.

"I have surveyed the area from the sky and found one dragon, the younger of the two and the one known as Raygon. She sleeps just the other side of those trees behind me but will awaken if you leave the cave because of a discovery spell placed which blocks your exit. You won't know if you break the unseen spell but it won't matter as she will and she will come at you with all rage and probably will not stop breathing fire until all that is left of you is ash, like in the hearth of a burnt-out fire."

"What do you suggest?" asked Yksboor, his mood darker because of what the bird had revealed to him.

"Leave it to me," said the bird. The bird was gone in the blink of an eye and was soon watching the sleeping dragon and waiting for the perfect time to launch his plan to help the knight escape.

Without realising it the dragon had been charmed by the bird, revealing the incantation to remove the discovery spell without even waking from its slumber.

The bird returned to the cave and sang what Yksboor believed to be more beautiful birdsong. What he did not know was that the bird had unlocked the invisible door to free him from the cave.

"Come, we must be quick, she will be awake soon as dragons never sleep long during the day or on an empty stomach," said the bird.

"And when she does wake up she will not be pleased one little bit. We had better make sure we are as far away as possible because her anger will be keen and she will want to kill anything in her path. If her mother discovers you are free she will want to punish her daughter and then she will also want to kill you. We must go far and very quickly if we are to help the people escape their terrible fate."

The bird started to fly away and Yksboor followed as quickly as he could, a steady run taking him along many paths as he attempted to keep pace with his guide and new-found companion.

The knight had asked Charlie to lead him to the Queen and the bird had told him to follow. Being out of his prison and feeling like he was able to at last do something worthwhile had filled his heart with joy and had given him real hope for the future.

Chapter 26

Livi and Dillon had stayed longer in the company of the old lady than they knew they really should.

But they had left with renewed optimism and love in their hearts. They wanted to believe they could do something good, something worthwhile which would help the Queen to win the war. They hoped, a hope which being with the old lady had given to them, not by anything she said but just by having them in her presence.

They had not been walking long when they saw a rider before them on a horse, riding at full speed through the long grass of the plain which lay in their path.

Joy leapt into the hearts of the companions. For it was the prince, but more importantly it was Livi's brother and she was glad above all else to see him again.

"Brother," she screamed with all of the breath in her lungs.

Upon hearing the cry, the prince reined in his horse and stopped. He looked across the plain for a few seconds in the direction of his sister and her faithful dog who were running in his direction. The smile on his sister's face was mirrored in the joyous look on the countenance of her brother.

A few brief moments were spent in hugs and kisses and Nathan was even treated to a dog-lick face wash from Dillon.

"Come, we must leave this place and go to our mother," said Nathan.

"But what of the knight?" asked Livi.

"I'm afraid we have to leave him to his own devices. I hope he can make his own escape and join us later. For now we have much more important work to do."

Nathan lifted his sister to join him in the saddle of his horse and set off at a gallop, the dog running swiftly at the side of the steed. As they rode Nathan revealed to his sister what their mother had discovered was her role, the most important thing she would probably ever have to do.

Livi and Nathan and Dillon had travelled several hours when they gave in to weariness and made their beds for the night in a sheltered clearing in an area of forest.

Nathan and Dillon slept lightly, both aware of the danger which could be lying close by. Only Livi got what you might call sleep, although she slept fitfully and was heard to murmur as she wriggled about as she lay on the hard ground. She woke to the noise of her brother and dog talking and joined them in a bland breakfast of wheat biscuits. They tasted hard and salty but all three knew they would get no more food that day as they had many miles still to travel.

Livi's thoughts were occupied with what her brother had told her. She knew the new task she had become aware of was a perilous one. She knew it would place her in danger and would take all of her strength, both physical and mental, but her determination grew more as she contemplated what she must do.

Chapter 27

Yksboor had little problem keeping pace with the bird as it moderated its pace so the knight was able to stay within sight. They had travelled a little over a day and were approaching an area called the Mountains of Mist as they were always shrouded in cloud. Charlie was about to swoop down and tell the knight it was time to rest when he saw something which made his heart sink. Riding across the plain behind them were what at first looked like a group of soldiers mounted on horses. Only they weren't soldiers and they weren't horses. They were goblins and the animals they rode were wolves, snarling and baring their teeth as they closed in on the knight who was making much slower progress on foot through the long grass.

Yksboor turned and looked in the direction of his pursuers, before turning to look back at the brightly coloured bird.

"I have to hide; I can't let anyone see me or know that I am here. I am sorry. If you escape I will return," said the bird.

Yksboor was not afraid, even though there were at least a dozen wolves bearing down on him at a heightened pace. Their riders were letting out crazed screams and waving curved swords over their heads. He had faced enemies many times in battle, fought in mortal combat to protect those he loved and those he had sworn to keep safe. He reached down to the scabbard fastened to his belt and withdrew the weapon. He had retrieved it from the cave where the dragons had carelessly tossed it amongst other treasures. They had marvelled at the workmanship and the jewels in the handle, ignoring the reason why it had been forged in the first place, to slay their kind.

Yksboor planted both feet slightly apart as he stood to face his enemies. He gritted his teeth and held the sword tip facing the floor in his right hand. He stared straight at his foes, his features held in a grim smile as he welcomed the chance at last to vent his anger. The bloodlust rose in him as the fear of the fight kept his wits on edge, tingling its way through his veins.

The first of the wolves reached Yksboor slightly before the rest and he cut its head straight from its shoulders with a swift strike, pulling the sword across his body as he moved his arm upwards and then swiftly striking down and across and out at the beast. The metal sliced through flesh and removed the animal's head from its shoulders, the wolf collapsing in a heap and the goblin being thrown at Yksboor's feet. The knight altered his grip on the sword and stabbed the blade down through the head of the goblin who let out a piercing scream, the last noise he would ever make.

Yksboor moved swiftly to face the remaining goblins who had leapt from their mounts and were forming themselves in a menacing semi-circle around the knight, the wolves pacing up and down behind their masters, salivating as they eyed the knight, ready to jump in and tear him limb from limb should the fight go against him.

Yksboor held his resolve as the goblins closed in, their curved swords arcing through the air as they made strokes and inched slowly towards their quarry.

The bravest, or as it turned out the most foolhardy, threw himself towards the knight and thrust forward with his sword, letting out a scream as he did so.

Yksboor dispatched the second goblin with a back-handed slap of the sword which crushed the goblin's skull, striking its helmet from on top of its head and sending it tumbling to the ground.

Yksboor turned to face the remaining goblins. Unlike men they had not fled in fear, instead their bloodlust had only been heightened by seeing two of their own killed right in front of their eyes. Luckily for the knight his bloodlust was more than a match for theirs, the desire to kill equally as much a driving force in his life as it was in theirs.

But perhaps the days he had spent in the cave had weakened him, that or some fowl incantation the dragons had used upon him. He was weary and did not see the blow from his extreme left, which struck his shoulder with the tip of the blade, the sword cutting through his halter top and slicing into his flesh. He turned his eyes to the wound, seeing the blue cloth turned a dark crimson. But no sound left his lips. There was no way he was going to be beaten, not the son of the Grand Knight Peter, the greatest of all the warriors to ply their trade in this or any other land.

Yksboor gritted his teeth once again and launched himself, striking out in all directions as his blows clattered against the blades of each of his opponents in turn.

They fought without break for what seemed like endless moments but as each of the goblins wearied Yksboor picked them off one by one until he was finally faced with one goblin. By now his opponent was too tired to fight on and Yksboor threw the sword straight at the goblin, the blade swinging end over end as it followed its true path to the head. The tip buried itself in the goblin's nose, splitting it to the bone and embedding itself in the flesh of the face, skin being peeled back and blood spurting like a fountain into the air.

With all of the goblins dead the remaining five wolves had a dilemma. They paced back and forth and then looked at each other before turning away, their tails tucked between their back legs in submission as they slunk away from the scene of destruction.

Yksboor had grown wearier the longer the fight went on. He knelt down on one leg and supported himself on the sword, gripping the handle to stop himself from collapsing in a heap on the ground. He was just collecting his thoughts, recovering his senses and trying to clear his troubled mind when he saw the bird land next to him.

"Ah, you're back now the work is done," said Yksboor as he wiped his sword's blade on the tunic of one of his dead opponents.

"Yes, I'm back as I said I would be. Congratulations on your art, you truly are a great swordsman. But enough of that, there is no time for congratulations. We must go. We are needed by the Queen; this battle might be won and the day saved but we have many more to fight and, hopefully, a war to win. Or better still, one to avert."

Yksboor rose to his feet and put his sword back in its scabbard before following the bird, taking the path into the lowest slopes of the nearest mountain.

Chapter 28

Smy couldn't believe he had been quite so stupid. He paced the room, his hands crossed behind his back as he thought what he could possibly do to get himself out of this particular predicament.

He had the prince securely locked down with the children but was horrified when he returned to check on his prize captures. The three children were still there, the two sisters and the boy, along with a selection of animals and other creatures which might have been animal in origin and might have been human in origin. Now most of them looked a mixture of the two, some half animal and half human, others half human and half animal. There was a unicorn, two centaurs and half a dozen mermaids, a narwhale, two lions and an elephant. All had started the normal size for those creatures and been shrunk after capture so Smy could fit them snugly and securely into his case.

But they were of little consequence to him when he realised the prince was missing; escaped. Smy had been preparing himself to hand over the prize capture to the wizard and had cursed himself many times for bragging of his capture before he had handed it over. He suspected the wizard already knew what he had to tell him or what he had been told by one of its servants. He was worried the wizard already knew what to expect Smy was about to reveal. But when he had to admit his prize had escaped Smy was filled with dread. To know that the knight had also got free from the dragons only served to double the wizard's anger, if that could be at all possible. They had been long and uncomfortable minutes as Smy had stood before the wizard, shifting nervously from one foot to the other. Most of the time had been silent for Smy as the wizard sat in his chair as if in a trance.

Finally the wizard had opened his eyes but the rage which burned inside made Smy lower his face in shame.

"I have learned that the knight has escaped. I think he had help from a bird, a creature in the form of a bird which represented a recently born male relative which filled his heart with hope and his muscles with strength," said the wizard.

"The dragons are angry, they want to kill and they will kill anything. I am angry and, I trust, you are angry to hear this news. Now, bring me good news so that I can be cheered."

"I fear I cannot," said Smy furtively.

The rage spread across the wizard's face and he cast a look at Smy which would have squeezed the breath out of many mortals. Smy blinked several times and tried to think of the next thing he should or could possibly say.

"Come, out with it," said an impatient wizard.

"The prince has escaped."

"What? How? How could you let this happen?"

"He was under a spell like the others, I guess he must have had help."

"You guess, is that the best you can come up with. This won't do, it's outside normal procedure. I want you to conduct a full investigation and deliver me a full report. Now, get out of my sight before I do something we might both regret, or even something which only you regret."

Smy didn't hang around. He knew when to make himself scarce and left the wizard's chamber, almost running along the corridor to his own room.

Smy pored over heavy books and manuscripts as he searched for the answer to the question. How could he recapture the prince and the knight and also get hold of the princess? It would take his strongest spells and all of his mental fortitude.

The best thing he could do was try to clear his mind and not allow thoughts of the wizard to get in the way of what he had to do. Smy began to feel better as he slipped into a deep trance and began to envisage what would happen if his plan came to fruition.

He saw a pack of wolves and goblin riders encircling the knight and, in the same valley, the two dragons swooping down over the prince and the princess, and that dog. In the centre of these two battles was the Queen, tied to a wooden stake. She looked dishevelled, her clothing torn and her head bowed, her blonde hair straggly and her face dirty. There were cuts to her face and bare shoulders.

What a pretty picture, Smy thought to himself. The wizard will be pleased.

All he needed to do was manipulate certain situations and he could ensure the scene would turn into reality.

Chapter 29

Yksboor followed the bird for many miles as they crossed slowly through rocky country. It was an easy passage for the bird but not for his companion. Yksboor's mind was still clouded by his ordeals at the mercy of the dragons and he still carried the shame that he had not been able to carry out his avowed purpose in life. He had dedicated his life to serve in the protection of the Queen and her country and felt terrible shame that he had been unable to do so, spending as he had done so much time in the country of dragons.

Elsewhere, not that far off, three other travellers were headed on a course which would bring them to the very same spot as Yksboor and Charlie at pretty much the very same time. Smy's plan was working out. He had sent out bands of goblins and had them harry both travelling parties incessantly until they chose the paths he wanted them to. One of the goblins had found what he needed to complete the final part of his plan. He had picked up a scarf which the princess had left behind when the goblins and wolves had attacked their resting place. They had been ordered not to capture anyone, just secure something which belonged to the princess. Something which could be used to tempt the Queen out of her castle so she could be captured and used as bait.

When she received the scarf and a note from Smy she had believed the words written there. The note, it said, was from a friend who had found Livi and Dillon and had helped them reach somewhere safe before sending word of where the Queen could find them. When she received the message the Queen held the scarf to her face and inhaled the scent of her daughter, the aroma she knew so well provoking an emotional response which resulted in a tear forming in the corner of her eye. She wiped it away with the back of her hand and went to make the preparations for her journey. She had followed the instructions in the note to travel alone and had taken a horse from the stable. Within three hours she was at the place where she had been told her daughter would be returned to her. But within minutes she realised something was terribly wrong. She was waiting in a hollow, hidden in some trees when her horse's ears pricked up and it snorted nervously. Movement all around the hollow alerted the Queen and she saw several heavily armed goblins push their way through the low tree branches. Two of them grabbed her and a third placed a cloth to her face, a strong smell overcoming her as she fought to remain conscious.

The Queen woke the next morning to find herself tied to a stake. Smy was stood smiling at her, flanked by two dragons and a whole host of goblins, some of them standing and others mounted on wolves.

"Ah, good Queen. Good day to you," said Smy.

"What's happening Smy, why am I here?" she demanded.

"I have a request for you. Do as I say and you and your loved ones will live. I need you to send word to your son and your daughter and to get them to surrender to the forces of the wizard. I assure you no harm will come to you or your family, or your people. Your country will be spared as long as it swears allegiance to the wizard. What is your answer?"

The Queen looked at him with contempt and spat in Smy's face. That was the only answer he was going to get.

The Queen had paid for her defiance. Under the instruction of Smy several goblins slapped her as she stood defenceless, tied to the stake in the clearing. Finally she had passed out. When she woke up the Queen was alone with Smy.

"Look over there," he said.

Livi, Nathan and Dillon stood at one end of the valley in the direction he was pointing.

"Now over there," said Smy, pointing to the other end of the valley. Yksboor was there.

The peace was broken by the blast of horns before the Queen had a chance to call out, to warn her family and the knight of what lay waiting for them. She looked at each end of the valley quickly. First she saw Livi and Nathan and the shock on their faces as they spotted her. As they moved forward they were stopped in their tracks by a screeching noise that was like metal grating on metal, a call she recognised as the cry of a dragon. The Queen's heart fell as she saw two dragons break cover from the trees on either side of the valley and fly over the children and the dog, forcing them to try to take cover as they scorched the earth with blasts of fire from their nostrils.

The Queen looked away, casting her eyes to the ground as her heart filled with uncontrollable pain.

When she looked up her eyes were drawn in the other direction. The knight was surrounded by at least twenty wolves, each carrying an armed goblin on its back. Some of them had bows and crossbows and the knight was already coming under a hail of arrows.

The Queen felt her heart grow heavier. She felt pain for her son and daughter, she felt pain for the dog, she felt pain for the knight. But most of all she felt pain for her people as she felt helpless to protect them.

As she bowed her head and waited for the end to come a thought crossed the Queen's mind. She thought back to what she had talked about with her son. Livi was the answer, the riddle's answer could save them all.

The Queen wanted to let Livi know but when she looked her daughter had been captured by one of the dragons, the girl's feet sticking out from under the dragon's foot as it pinned her to the ground. Desperately the Queen called out to her son.

"Nathan, Nathan," she shouted.

The prince was using all of his skill to fend off the younger dragon, aided by Dillon who had his jaws locked into the dragon's tail as it was swished this way and that in a bid to shake him off.

The prince looked at the Queen as the dragon took off and finally shook the dog off, Dillon crashing into a tree before falling to the floor and lying motionless on the scorched earth.

Black, acrid smoke filled the air in the valley and Nathan had to peer through it to see his mother. He cocked his head to one side so he could concentrate on what she was trying to shout to him.

"It's Livi, get her to sing. She must sing!"

Nathan realised what his mother wanted. He evaded the dragon as it swooped down and ran towards the larger animal, arcing his sword over his head and bringing the weapon down crashing across the dragon's foot which had his sister trapped underneath it. A piercing scream filled the air and the dragon reeled back, lifting the foot off the princess. Livi seized the moment and jumped to her feet, running to her brother and burying her head in his chest as she gripped him in a fierce hug.

"Listen to me Livi," he said as he gripped Livi by the shoulders and looked into her eyes.

Livi broke into a happy song and the result was instantaneous. Both dragons gazed at her with puzzled looks on their faces but that soon turned to pained stares. The dragons screeched in unison, the noise much worse than the one the mother had made when Nathan had slashed his sword across her foot.

Soon the pain became unbearable for both dragons and they swooped up into the air before flying away from the valley.

Nathan and Livi ran to the Queen and the prince quickly and skilfully cut her bonds. Free of her ties she hugged her daughter and kissed her on the head before turning to face her son.

"We have to help him," said the Queen as she turned to look at the knight who was keeping the goblins at bay, a number of them lying dead at his feet along with the wolves they had ridden.

The knight looked at the Queen and her children and motioned for them to leave and the Queen and Nathan knew what he intended was the right thing for them to do.

The Queen put an arm around the shoulder of each of her children and they started to walk away but she realised Livi was crying.

"Where's Dillon?" asked the girl.

As if in response the dog raised itself up on its four legs and barked. Livi, realising he was alive, ran to him and wrapped her arms around him, nuzzling her cheek against his.

Nathan and his mother allowed the girl a very brief moment to be together with her dog before they herded them out of the valley.

At the other end of the valley Yksboor continued to toil in his battle. Now just four goblins and six wolves remained from the forty creatures he had faced.

When he had realised the battle was going against him Smy had retreated to the safety of the forest. He watched the Queen leave the valley with her children and cast a cursory glance towards the knight. He snorted derisively and kicked the wolf he was sat on hard in its rib cage. The wolf grumbled loudly enough for its rider to hear then obeyed the command as it ran swiftly through the trees. Smy was angry; his plan had seemed perfect and had looked to be playing out. Until the Queen and the princess intervened. He would make them both pay for that and turned his thoughts to revenge as the wolf carried him over the forest floor.

Later when Smy stopped to rest he was horrified when he opened his briefcase to find the boy and the sisters were missing. They had somehow escaped, perhaps when he was distracted during the battle. His mood deepened and he felt utterly miserable.

Chapter 30

The Queen sat with her legs crossed talking to her son as the princess and Dillon lay together sleeping nearby. The young girl had been worn out by the day's events and her heavy breathing was matched like an echo by the snoring of the dog.

The Queen smiled as she looked at the two of them and turned to her son.

"I have no idea what we do now," she said.

"Everything I do seems to be wrong and leads us into more danger. Maybe we should just forget about everything here and look for a new land to live in. I am tired of ruling and of this war, I just want to be able to look after you and Livi and forget everything else."

"You can't do that mother," replied her son.

"Everyone relies on you, they are looking to you to save them. You are their ruler. Besides, you know it is Livi's destiny. She must do this."

The Queen sighed in resignation.

"I know, but that doesn't make it any easier to accept. She will be put in great danger. Both of you will. I can't bear the thought of losing either one of you."

Nathan checked his sword in the scabbard before rising to his feet.

"You must stop worrying about what you cannot change," he said.

"Now, get some sleep. I will take first watch and then wake Dillon during the night to take over from me."

Chapter 31

The knight placed his foot on the wolf's ribcage and gripped his sword with both hands before yanking it free from the dead animal.

He looked about him and surveyed nothing but death. Already the foul stench of it filled the air and it made his nostrils sting as he fought to catch his breath and recover from his exertions.

The knight had fought hard and suffered many injuries. He was exhausted and his soul felt empty. His life was dedicated to killing but each time he took a life something within him died. He had no choice but to fight to protect those he was sworn to defend but he did not enjoy taking lives.

He stood there with his head bowed and wondered how long he could keep up this sort of life.

He wanted no part of it, not since he had taken the first life when he was not much more than a boy. But he knew he had no choice. This life had been chosen for him by his birth and it was a life he dedicated himself to out of honour, even if he derived no pleasure from it. But he knew he had little time to dwell upon it as more battles, and more killing, lay ahead.

Yksboor took his time to pile the bodies of the goblins and the beasts and started a fire. At least they could have some semblance of a good send-off. He watched the fire take hold then replaced his sword in its scabbard which was supported by the belt that he wore across his shoulder and around his body, which would make travelling that bit more comfortable. He had taken food from his dead enemies and gave them one last, lingering glance in return before turning and walking to the nearest trees.

Once inside the cover of the forest he began running, drawing on reserves of strength not even he knew he had.

Several hours later he laid his head to sleep after taking cover in a clump of bushes, trusting to his skill in finding a secluded spot to keep him safe from prying eyes.

Chapter 32

The Queen had reached the safety of her home with her children and she was grateful they were all safe.

She picked up a map and studied it before lifting her head and staring out of the window to the drifts of black smoke which rose from several places in the far distance. The evil forces of the wizard and witch were wreaking havoc upon the land, the evil lord and the dragons leading raiding parties which killed and pillaged as they went. People were losing heart and the Queen knew they would soon face a pivotal battle in the war to rid the kingdom of invading forces.

As she stood there the Queen let out a long sigh and bowed her head. Deep in thought, she did not notice her daughter walk up behind her.

"Mummy, what is wrong?" asked the young girl.

The Queen turned to hold her daughter and kissed her on the forehead. The time had come to tell the princess that she held the secret which could save the kingdom.

But the Queen knew to make it work she would have to place herself and her daughter in mortal danger. There was no guarantee it would work and every chance it would actually prove no more than mere folly.

The Queen placed her arm around her daughter's shoulder as they walked together out of the bedroom door and through the corridors of the castle.

As they walked the Queen told Livi she would have to be very brave as, in order to make her plan work they would have to be separated.

The Queen told her daughter about the riddle and of her discovery that Livi held the secret to their salvation. She told Livi the only way they could win was if the girl was to whistle her tune and that would help them defeat the wizard and the witch and spare the people any more misery and suffering.

The Queen had decided she would have to put a plan into action which would see her be the decoy in order for Livi to get the chance to succeed.

"Is she ready?" asked the prince.

"Yes she is, but I don't think I am," replied the Queen.

"I know she must do this but I can't help feeling it will fail. And if it does then all is lost. What if we were to just leave and save ourselves? Or perhaps we could throw ourselves upon the mercy of the wizard."

Nathan let out a grim laugh. He said: "We will be shown no mercy. All that will happen is we be killed and so will all of your people who do not obey the wizard. And even then he will probably have them all slaughtered anyway."

Chapter 33

The evil lord looked up at the walls of the castle and shrugged his shoulders. He had never seen a creature that could scale such a height, let alone a man.

"Fetch him to me," he said, turning to his captain.

"Yes, my lord," replied the captain.

A scraggly man of about twenty-one was hustled to the front of the waiting crowd of soldiers.

"Right. You don't look like you could climb a fence, how can I be sure you can climb into the castle and steal the princess?" he asked.

"Give me the gold I was promised and you will see," replied the cocky young man, the moon glinting off a gold tooth in the corner of his mouth as he smiled wickedly.

"They call you Tom, right? Well, Tom, if you do this for me you will be rewarded beyond your wildest dreams. The wizard himself will be in your debt."

Tom needed no more encouragement. He climbed dextrously up the fifty feet to the window of the princess's bedroom. He had been told the dog would not be with her tonight, information provided by a source inside the castle who had been bought by the power of a handful of gold coins.

Tom reached the window in a matter of minutes and climbed silently through. He tiptoed over to the bed and watched the young girl sleeping. It puzzled him how she could be so important. Why didn't the wizard just smash his way into the castle? He removed the coil of rope from over his shoulder which he would use to lower the girl down the castle wall. Next he took the sack from his belt which he would put over her head and the length of twine he would use to bind the sack tightly so she could not escape from it.

He was just about to reach for the girl when a sound startled him. The bedroom door was opened and there stood the prince. He drew his sword and stepped silently into the room. Tom drew a long-bladed dagger from his belt and they squared up. The prince made the first lunge but it was easily parried by Tom who had learnt his skills fighting for survival on the streets and in the taverns of the city. To test them against such a fine swordsman as the prince was something he never imagined would happen but it was an honour he welcomed. Taking the prince's ring finger back with him would not only prove to the lord what he had done but also provide him with bragging rights amongst his cohorts. And the ring would sell for a high price too.

But Nathan had no intention of giving up his finger and even less intention of allowing his sister to be taken, or worse killed. He redoubled his efforts and they fought, each taking the lead to strike blows which were parried. Then Tom went for what he thought would be the killer move. He used his free hand to reach for a smaller dagger which he kept at his back, tucked under his belt. His ploy would have been deadly for many but Nathan had expected such a move and grabbed the man's wrist, digging the nail of his thumb into the flesh until the man squealed in pain and dropped the dagger. Nathan bent swiftly and picked up the dagger, parrying the other blade with his sword and rising to strike a blow into the man's chest. As his assailant reeled back against a chair Nathan hacked off his other hand with a powerful blow. He stood there breathing heavily before glancing at his sister who, miraculously, was still sleeping. How could Livi sleep through that, he wondered.

He picked up the hand, still clutching the dagger, and wrapped it inside the man's tunic and lifted the body before carrying it over to the window. He pushed the body out of the window and waited until he heard the thud as it landed on the grass below.

The lord walked over to where the body lay face down and gave it a cursory push with his boot so he could see the face of the burglar.

"Too cocky," he said. "Still, it was worth a try. Tomorrow we face them in battle and soon we will by feasting in the castle's Great Hall. Come men."

The evil lord led his small party of men off to some nearby trees where they untethered their horses and rode off.

Chapter 34

The Queen called out her son's name and he walked over to her.

"What is it mother?" he asked.

"It's Livi. I can't wake her. It's as if she's in a trance. You will have to face the battle without us. I must stay with her. If she wakes up I will bring her to you."

The prince rubbed his chin, lost in thought.

"If that is how it must be," he said. "Perhaps that intruder I killed had time to poison her. As long as she lives there is hope."

The prince mounted his horse and led his guard out of the castle gates.

The Queen returned to her daughter's side and mopped her fevered brow with cold water as physicians stood around consulting textbooks and arguing about the best way to treat the princess.

Livi was unaware of the work going on around her to find a cure to her malaise. She was in a deep sleep but her mind was definitely awake. In her unconscious mind she was running through a dark forest as many creatures screeched and swooped about her, trying to dig their sharp talons into her back. Several times she thought they had caught her only for them to swoop away as if they weren't really trying to grab her at all. Their intentions became clear as she stumbled into a clearing where she was faced by a large wolf lying on the ground and surrounded by the bones of hundreds of bodies.

"Welcome, I have been expecting you," said the wolf.

The wolf stared at the girl for several seconds before either of them spoke, the atmosphere dark as the girl had thoughts of escape and the wolf had thoughts of capture and many things much worse.

"What do you want of me?" asked Livi.

"What do I want? I want you to die and then I want you to be my next meal. Although, looking at you, it won't do much to satisfy my appetite," replied the wolf as she raised herself up and stretched, yawning to show her rows of saliva-dripped fangs.

Livi gulped and tried to think of what she would do to escape from the wolf.

Chapter 35

Joshua surveyed the valley from the cover of the trees. He had lined his five hundred archers in rows in the clearing so they had a clean line of fire at the valley. However, he knew that if they were attacked they would be vulnerable and would find it difficult to defend themselves.

Joshua had been drawn into this battle against his will. His skill as a bowman had led to approaches from both sides to go into paid service. He had previously rejected the advances of both the king and the evil lord, preferring to eke out his existence as a farmer with his family. But the actions of the lord's cohorts had forced his hand. On the day it happened he was at market with his son Joe selling cattle and had returned to find his farmhouse on fire. His wife and daughter were both slain, along with every animal on the farm. Joshua and Joe had both taken an oath to avenge their women folk and joined the Queen's forces.

Joshua now found himself commanding the archers but having Joe at his shoulder at least gave him the comfort of knowing his son was safe, as long as he was close.

As Joshua looked out on the battlefield he knew things were stacked against the side he had chosen to fight for. The prince stood at the head of five thousand men, most of them professional soldiers but a good number of farmers like Joshua. They were faced by a force of at least three times as many men and beasts. There were the soldiers of the lord's employ: mercenaries, goblins mounted on wolves and, most frightening of all, the two dragons. There were also a number of Fighting Giants and their reputation as fierce fighters was known far and wide and their presence filled many of the Queen's men with fear and dread.

Stood behind the enemy forces on a small hill were the wizard and the witch, a dragon sat either side of them.

The wizard turned to the witch and laughed.

He said, "Soon we will be feasting in the castle."

He nodded to the evil lord and gave the signal to the leader of the goblins and the captain of the horse who both simultaneously gave the order for their forces to charge.

Hordes of men on horse and wolf-mounted goblins charged into the valley and towards the prince's forces.

When they reached a stake which had been driven into the earth five hundred yards from the first of the prince's forces, Joshua gave the order and the first row of archers released a volley of arrows. They knelt to load another arrow into their bows and the second row of archers fired. Then the third, fourth and fifth rows. Each volley landed with brutal force into the charging men and goblins and their mounts. Wave after wave of them fell to the ground.

Alarmed by the way his men were being slaughtered the lord ordered the retreat to be sounded and a man blew the call on a horn. As the cavalry and goblins retreated to the lord he gathered the forces around him and then led a charge back into the valley but this time they headed for the trees where the archers were hidden. Many of the men and goblins fell but several hundred made it to the cover of the trees and rushed through them to seek out the archers. Joshua had expected such an attack and, under cover of the previous night, had ordered his men to dig pits which were covered with branches. The leading horses and wolves feel into the pits where they and their riders were impaled on large stakes which had been driven into the ground.

Yet still the lord's forces charged on and soon they were upon the archers and a fierce battle of close contact ensued. Many of the archers were killed or injured before the prince led his own cavalry into the trees and they forced the remainder of the attackers to flee.

Joshua looked about him and saw several friends dead and injured. He looked at the prince and his grim face told its own story.

"How bad is it?" asked the prince.

"I have lost maybe two hundred men but don't worry. We will be ready the next time they come and we will take many with us."

"Thank you," replied the prince as he led his cavalry back to the ranks of his main force.

Yksboor surveyed the battle from the shade of a tree as the midday soon rose towards its nadir. He was mounted on a horse and at the head of a group of around forty horsemen who had rallied to him as he headed back towards the castle. He had come upon the battle around five minutes before and sat in his saddle watching as the lord led the remnants of his attack back to his lines. Yksboor turned to the bird sat on a nearby branch.

"You know what must be done," said Charlie.

"And you, what will you do?" replied Yksboor.

"I will wait here until you are finished."

Yksboor took the bow from across his shoulder and tested the string. The weapon had been well made and the arrow would fly true. Yksboor called the other horsemen to him and explained what he wanted to do.

The horsemen started slowly and then began to gallop towards the hill where the wizard, the witch and the two dragons were watching the battle as it unfolded. Several skirmishes were taking place on the edge of the woods and their attention was fixed on one place or another. Yksboor was hidden within the group of horsemen but from there he could see both dragons had switched their gaze upon his party as they approached to within about five hundred feet. Yksboor stood up in the saddle and took careful aim, in the same way he had been taught to fire from the saddle by the people of the east with the narrow eyes who had visited his father many years before. When they were within about a hundred feet, Yksboor released the arrow which flew straight and true and into the eye of Raygon. The arrow found its target with such force that it went straight through the eye socket and buried itself into the brain of the dragon, killing the creature instantly. Raygon collapsed and her mother let out a piercing scream which caused all of the fighting men and beasts to turn. The noise was so piercing that even the servants in the castle more than a mile away stopped what they were doing and looked in the direction of the battlefield.

Tremgara raised herself up on her back legs and forced a blast of fire from her nostrils. She flapped her great wings and took off, swooping high into the sky before swinging down on the group of horsemen. As she sped down she sent another blast of fire from her nostrils, setting several horses and men on fire and scattering the remainder.

Chapter 36

The scream of the dragon had startled the Queen but had not woken the princess from her trance. The Queen looked at her daughter and offered a silent prayer to the gods. The physicians continued to argue over what was wrong with the princess and what was the best way to treat her.

Livi was oblivious to what was happening around her as she had other things to occupy her mind.

She stood at the edge of the clearing and looked the wolf straight in the eyes. Inside she was petrified but knew she could not show any fear. If she did the wolf would sense it and her fate would be sealed. Livi spent seconds, which seemed like hours, trying to come up with a way out of the clearing with her life intact. Her determination was borne out of a desire to help her mother save the kingdom as much as for her own safety.

The wolf raised itself up and began to circle the girl slowly, looking for an opening to attack its prey. As the wolf walked around her, Livi turned round so she could keep the animal in front of her at all times. Much as she tried to keep calm Livi knew she was shaking with fear and had to concentrate her mind to stop herself from falling to her knees and crying out in anguish.

The wolf started to smile to herself when she saw the girl was afraid. She could smell the fear and the smell excited her as hunger raged in her belly and killing the girl would satisfy that need as much as the need to taste blood. She started to move slowly to the girl and was amazed to see when she sank to her knees and buried her head in her hands. The wolf walked up to the girl and started to sniff at her hair. She could not see the girl's face but the sniffing noise she was making meant she was crying. It would not be long before she was begging for mercy and after that she would become a tasty meal.

Livi moved with a swiftness that startled even her. She picked up the bone from her side and thrust the broken end into the wolf's shoulder. The startled wolf leapt back and shrieked in pain. Livi took her moment and started to sing. The wolf, already badly injured, could not take the sweet sounds and cowered in a corner of the clearing. Livi finished the song and walked over to the wolf. She put out her hand and stroked the animal on the shoulder near the wound. The wolf, which at first started to growl, lowered its head in complicity and licked the girl's hand. It looked at the wound and saw, to its amazement, that it had healed. The wolf looked at the girl and said; "Go, return from where you came. You and all you love are welcome in my lands and protected by my kind. You are my friend."

Livi opened her eyes and looked into those of her mother's.

"Oh, Livi, you are back. Thank the gods," said the Queen.

Livi looked at the other people crowding around her bed and staring at her.

"What are all these people doing?" she asked.

"They're here to help. But that doesn't matter, we have more important things to worry about."

Chapter 37

Dillon stood in the doorway and barked excitedly.

"Dillon, Dillon," cried the girl.

The dog jumped up on to the bed and rushed at Livi, his body shaking from side to side as he licked her face.

"It's good to see you are back with us my princess," he said.

"It's good to be back. I have been on an adventure but I will tell you of that later. First my mother has important things for us to do, so she tells me."

"Yes, the battle rages and we are no nearer winning. In fact, if a miracle doesn't happen very soon I fear our forces will be defeated."

The Queen took the time to again patiently tell Livi what she must do and also beseeched Dillon to protect his friend as the mission was most vital to the future prosperity of the people. Dillon agreed and promised he would, as always, remain faithful in his duty to protect the princess.

Chapter 38

The dragon had scattered the group of riders who had attacked but had not found the one responsible for killing her daughter. Her rage burned deep within her heart and she was determined to avenge the death of Raygon by killing any creature she came across. The dragon had flown the mile or so – a short distance to her and only several beats of her powerful wings – to the castle where people and animals scattered before her. She swooped down several times on the castle and burned everything her foul breath could come into contact with. Time and again she came out of the sky and grabbed a person or cattle in her talons before releasing them against the castle walls. She also picked up large boulders from outside the castle walls and bombed the buildings where people were taking shelter.

The Queen guided her daughter and the dog around several winding passageways in the bowels of the castle. Deeper they went underground but their ears were not protected from the roar of the dragon or the panicked screams of the humans and animals it pursued relentlessly above them.

More than once the Queen stopped to listen carefully to make sure none had seen them enter the tunnel or followed them there. This way was secret and its existence had been passed down by word of mouth from one ruler of the castle to the next. It was not that the Queen did not want her people to be safe but she could not risk the tunnel being discovered as she might need to use it to return to the castle later if something went wrong with her plan.

Eventually their way was lit by light at the end of the tunnel and the Queen was able to extinguish the torch she had been carrying. They appeared into the light and found themselves at the foot of a hill. At the other side of the hill they could hear the battle raging; the cries of men and beasts, the clash of swords and the shrill trumpet of horns. In the distance they could tell the dragon was still attacking the castle and roared as it continued to wreak its havoc.

The Queen took the lead, Dillon and Livi following her, as she climbed to the top of the hill. From this vantage point they were able to see the field before them littered with dead bodies. All about lay men and beasts, some of them dead, others dying and yet more wounded. It pained the Queen to see such death in her land but she forced that thought from her mind as she stole herself for what she had to ask her daughter to do.

She knelt down in front of her daughter and gripped her by the shoulders, looking straight into her eyes and speaking in a slow and calm voice.

"Livi, listen to me, you are the most precious thing to me in the whole of my lands, more important than being the Queen or ruling over the subjects, more important than any wealth I have or any wealth I could imagine. Are you ready for what you must do?"

"Yes mother," came the girl's reply, accompanied by a broad smile.

"I need you to whistle your favourite tune. I don't know why it is you or why you have to whistle. I only know that it is you and that you must whistle. You must focus your total attention on this and not be distracted. Do not worry about anything else as Dillon and I will be here to protect you. Do not worry about us as we will be safe. Is this clear?"

"Yes mother, it's clear."

The Queen moved behind her daughter and placed a hand on each shoulder. Dillon lay at the girl's feet and kept his eyes fixed on the battlefield.

Chapter 39

Nathan looked over his shoulder, instinct telling him that his mother and sister were close. At the end of the valley he could see them on top of the hill along with Dillon. He knew he had to distract attention away from them and issued a rallying call to the cavalry close to him. When he had gathered around a hundred men he rode over to where Joshua was expertly guiding the bowmen to direct their arrows for maximum effect.

"I need to create a diversion," said Nathan.

"What for? This battle will be over soon and we will have lost. There is nothing we can do to win the battle and, besides, there is nothing left worth fighting for."

"Please, just help me. I can't explain why but if what I think may happen does happen the battle will be over in our favour. If not, then what have we got to lose? I beg of you, please help me."

Joshua thought about what to do. In his mind he could see his wife and daughter collecting corn in the field, then he saw his slaughtered animals and burning farm buildings. Next to him his boy moved and Joshua looked into his eyes, seeing the answer to what he must do in them.

"Ok, what must we do?" he asked of the prince.

"I need you to place some of your men in front of the trees so they can protect my horsemen as we ride towards the wizard. I am to kill him, or the witch or at worst take one of them prisoner."

"That's a fool's errand but I will not question the wisdom of it."

Nathan smiled and led his men to the edge of the trees where they waited for the bowmen to take up position.

The horsemen charged to the hill where the wizard stood with the witch as they viewed the battlefield, a small group of goblins keeping guard. A volley of arrows fell on the ranks of goblins at the rear of the wizard's forces, keeping them occupied as the prince led his horsemen behind them and towards the hill.

The wizard was the first to see the approaching horsemen and alerted his guard. The goblins quickly mounted their wolves and charged at the prince and his forces, smashing into them with a terrible crash as men and beasts collided. The prince and his men became engaged in hand-to-hand combat and many men, goblins and beasts fell to the earth. Some lay dead and others dying as the cries of the wounded filled the air.

The wizard shifted his attention away from the horsemen who were engaged in a fierce fight and fixed his gaze on the bowmen who were harrying those of his goblins trying to help their comrades in the fight against the prince's men. He gave the order to one of his captains and he rode off to ranks of goblins who were held in reserve behind the hill. A large group of goblins rode forward before splitting into two smaller groups. The first surrounded the prince and his men while the others charged at the bowmen. Both fights lasted what must have been half an hour before the prince was finally captured. Joshua and his son had refused to surrender and were the last of the bowmen to be slaughtered, shot with the weapons of their comrades as they tried to fight on with only swords in their hands.

As Nathan saw Joshua fall under a volley of arrows he lowered his head and sank to his knees. He was dragged across the field and made to kneel before the wizard and the witch.

"Ha, the prince kneels before me and my beloved," said the wizard.

"I knew this day would come. A pity you could not have saved so much bloodshed by kneeling before me sooner. What was that little foolish game about? What did you hope to achieve by trying to attack me? You must have known it was madness."

"Madness is what you suffer from, old man," replied the prince defiantly. "You will be the loser this day and you will be driven from these lands."

"I don't think so," said the wizard. "You and your mother will both kneel before me. Your father foolishly banished me from this land and I swore that day I would return to seek my retribution. I will be king and rule over this land. You and your family will be sold into slavery. Anyone who does not acquiesce will pay the ultimate price with their miserable lives being forfeit. Take him away."

The prince was hauled to his feet by two goblins and taken away to be held with the remainder of his horsemen who had survived the fight.

Chapter 40

Yksboor had seen the prince captured but was busy avoiding the attentions of the dragon who was circling over the valley. She was intent on killing him and he was intent on avoiding that. He knew he needed to draw the dragon away from the battle but that meant using himself as bait. He chose to make for the woods and made sure the dragon was able to see where he was going. Once he reached the treeline he got off his horse and hid behind a large rock. If the dragon caught him in the open he knew it would not last long and he would be the loser.

The dragon swooped low over the trees as she searched for her prey.

"Come out and face me knight," she bellowed. "You killed my daughter and I will do the same to you. Come and face me or are you afraid?"

Chapter 41

The prince and his men were being escorted from the field but luckily they had not been bound in chains. At the first chance he gave the signal to his captain and they both lunged at the nearest guards. The prince's other men joined in the escape and they soon overpowered their guards. After checking their escape had not been detected by the wizard's forces, they made their way back to where the Queen and the princess were being protected by the palace guard. They were under attack by the lord and his guard and welcomed the new men who joined their ranks.

The prince went to his mother's side and looked in anguish at her after seeing his sister standing in a trance.

"It's ok, she has to do this," said the Queen. "I know it's a risk but she is the one chosen to do this for my people. I only hope she can come through it."

The Queen took her son's hand in hers and squeezed tightly as they both looked at the princess.

Chapter 42

Yksboor looked across at his dying horse. The petrified animal had run off and ventured into open ground where the dragon had swooped down. It had gripped the beast in its claws, sinking the talons into the flesh before swooping up into the sky. The dragon dropped the animal and it crashed off the rock which Yksboor was hiding behind. The knight could barely look at the animal as it lay yards away, thrashing around in pain. He dare not move to put it out of its misery as the dragon would get the chance to attack him. He had to wait his time but doing so was agony for him, seeing the poor animal in pain and having to listen to it as the life slowly ebbed from it.

The knight gathered his thoughts and struck out for the nearest trees. He crossed the small piece of open ground and stood with his back to the tree, breathing heavily. He watched as the dragon circled around the clearing and then ran through the trees. The dragon saw him break cover into open ground and turned down towards her prey, screaming her triumph as she closed in on the man.

Yksboor stopped and turned to face the dragon, drawing his sword as he placed both feet firmly and waited for the dragon to attack. As the dragon swopped down the knight moved aside and managed to avoid its outstretched claws, striking a blow against its leg. But all that did was send a shock through his arm and it was all he could do to hold on to the sword. He turned to face the dragon as it came at him again but this time was not quick enough to avoid the blow as it kicked out at him. The blow caught the knight full in the chest and he was sent barrelling backwards over the ground. The knight slowly got to his feet and shook his head as he tried to make sense of what had happened. He could hear the dragon flapping its wings as it circled above him and he waited for its next attack, setting himself ready for the blow.

Chapter 43

The Queen looked at her daughter and then to her son. She knew time was short and she had to act now; it was a difficult decision but she knew she had no other choice.

She knelt in front of her daughter and gripped her by the shoulders, starting to gently shake her. There was no response from the girl who was still in a trance. The Queen started to shake more violently but nothing seemed to stir the girl from her state.

"What are you doing Mother? You'll hurt her," said the prince.

"I have to wake her. We must leave this place. There is no time. We must seek safety."

The girl opened her eyes and looked her mother straight in the eyes and said: "I have failed. I am sorry."

The Queen put her arm around her daughter's shoulder and led her away from the battlefield. The prince and his remaining men formed a guard around the Queen and her daughter.

The princess stopped for a moment and looked across the field where she saw the bodies of dead and dying men and beasts. Among all of the fallen she saw the body of a young boy she recognised. It was William. After he had escaped from Smy he had sought out men from his village in the Queen's army. He had joined with them and, as tales would later tell, had fought with great courage and no thought for his own safety. He was one of many who died that day and the princess knew she had to stay safe and defeat the wizard and the witch so that the sacrifices made by so many were not wasted.

Tears started to stream down the girl's face as she thought of the boy she had known all too briefly and the bravery he had shown.

Chapter 44

Yksboor knew the end was close. He could feel the weight of the dragon bearing down on him and there was nothing he could do. He was pinned by the dragon's foot and was unable to move. A feeling of bitter regret swept through his mind and he felt totally helpless because he knew there was nothing he could do about it. He looked the beast straight in the eye with a stare which all but begged the beast to finish him. The look he got in return was one of pure malevolence.

Yksboor closed his eyes and prepared for the end when he felt the pressure on his chest relax. He looked up to see the dragon had turned its head and was looking back towards the battle.

The dragon turned back to face the knight and said, "I will finish with you later."

With one beat of its wings the beast lifted off and swept away, screeching loudly as it did so.

Yksboor rose to his feet and collected his weapon before walking to the nearest trees and disappearing.

The wizard stood alone, waiting for the dragon to approach. The beast swept down and landed next to the wizard, lowering its head so it could hear what he had to say.

"The Queen takes flight. I want you to follow her. I will send goblins to harry their progress before you find out where they are going. When the time is right you will kill all of them. Then you can deal with the knight."

"Then I will deal with the knight," said Tremgara with a wicked grin.

Chapter 45

The prince entered the camp and dismounted his weary horse. The animal was breathing hard and its rider was equally as exhausted. The prince warmed his hands in front of the fire before sitting next to his mother.

"Will we make it to The Hiding Tree?" she asked.

"I hope so. But it's strange. Each time I think we are going to be captured they pull back. Something is wrong. It's like they don't want to capture us. Maybe they are waiting for the right time."

"Nothing surprises me with the wizard. It's probably just one of his tricks. I'm sure he will have some evil plan for us. Sometimes I just wish it could be over. If I could just take you two away with me so we could be safe somewhere I would give everything up."

"You know that's not possible, Mother."

Their escape took two days and two nights but eventually they came close to their destination.

The camp awoke to the sounds of blood-curdling screams. Arrows crashed against the trees and several men were hit, falling to the ground and crying out in pain.

The prince charged at the nearest goblin and slashed his sword across its throat. A second goblin charged to meet him and was met with a roundhouse blow which removed its arm at the elbow. But the prince knew there were too many of them. It was when he heard the scream of a dragon and looked through the canopy of the trees to see the beast circling above that he realised all was lost. But despite that he charged straight at the enemy, striking blows at each adversary he came across.

The Queen had pulled her daughter close to her and with her other hand she held a sword, ready to fight off anyone who threatened the most precious thing in her life. The goblins were getting closer and the Queen could see the dragon had landed in a clearing and had set fire to the trees behind them. Soon the fire and the goblins would have them trapped and they would have to surrender or be slaughtered.

A blinding flash of light lit up the sky.

The Queen awoke with a splitting headache. She was laid on a bed and she could hear shallow breathing next to her. She looked to see her daughter lying next to her. At the end of the bed her son was sleeping in an armchair.

Two girls were stood to one side of the bed.

"Hello my Queen, welcome to our home," said the older girl.

"My name is Hattie and this is my sister Millie. She was the one who saved you. And this is where we live, this is…

"This is The Hiding Tree," said the Queen, finishing the sentence for the girl.

"Yes. This is The Hiding Tree. You are all perfectly safe here."

The Queen looked to the other side of the bed where Dillon was stretched out asleep in front of a roaring fire. The dog's paws were twitching and he was uttering smothered yelps.

'Oh what joy it must be to be able to dream of chasing rabbits,' thought the Queen to herself.

"Do you think there is any way we can stop the wizard?" asked the younger girl, Millie.

"Yes. I think there might be," replied the Queen. "Listen, girls, I have a plan. The princess can stop the wizard, but she needs time to be able to do that. The only way it can work is if Millie can be there to protect her. Millie, can you do it?"

"I think so. But I want Hattie there. If she is holding my hand I won't be afraid. Will you be there?"

"Of course I will," replied the Queen.

Chapter 46

The wizard stood on top of the hill and surveyed the valley. Several weeks had passed since he had been cheated of his prize. The Queen had gathered all the reinforcements she could and had been hemmed into this valley by his combined armies.

The dragon circled the valley before landing next to the wizard.

"All is ready. The time has come for it to end," she said.

"Yes. Soon the kingdom will be mine. And you will have the knight."

"And I will have the knight."

The noise of drums and horns filled the valley as the two armies marched towards each other. Men and beasts marched beside each other, riders whipping their mounts to keep them facing in the direction of the slaughter. The Queen's forces were greatly outnumbered but she was too busy to worry about that. She had left her son in charge of leading the troops as she hurried with her daughter and the two sisters to the place she had chosen. It was a small mound to the right of the valley and, she hoped, far enough away from the wizard not to be noticed.

The wizard knew the Queen would have a plan and had sent his scouts out to look for her. For several days they had searched without success and had reported nothing of her movements. But he knew she would have to risk her daughter if she was to have any chance of winning the battle. And he would be waiting.

The prince surveyed the battlefield from his horse. He commanded a force of around 10,000 men who had been gathered from the farthest reaches of the land. The promise of reinforcements from neighbouring kingdoms could have swelled their ranks by at least as many more but so far that was all it was, a promise. The wizard had at least three times as many men and beasts at this command and also the dragon. The beast was flying high in the sky above them, waiting for the right moment to swoop down and scatter all before it through fear alone.

Cedric was a captain in the Queen's guard and stood with his men in front of the mound. He would rather be in the thick of the fight but he had his orders. He looked down the line of his men and knew they would hold as long as was necessary. He also knew they would fight to the death to protect the Queen and the princess.

"This is the day. This is the day we have waited for. Make it yours," Cedric said to his men.

"Give no quarter, for your enemies will spare you no mercy. Fight and fight to the end. Leave nothing behind here today."

The Queen smiled as she heard Cedric's words. His father had been the captain of her father's guard and she knew she could rely on him.

At the other end of the valley Elfrud looked along the line of goblins as they marched towards the battle. He was pleased with what he saw. They were several thousand stronger than the enemy but he expected a fierce battle. And that was what he wanted. He felt the adrenaline course through his body as he anticipated the slaughter ahead. For too long he had been denied the chance to revenge his fallen comrades. He wanted to kill and he would like nothing more than to take a prize scalp. That of the prince, or the knight. Nobody had heard of the knight since the previous battle and many in the wizard's army had called him coward. Elfrud knew better. He knew the knight would be back and he wanted to be the one to kill him. Only then would he feel he had honoured his own father who had fought many battles in the service of the wizard. Today would only be a good day if he killed the knight. Winning the battle would be easy but it mattered little to Elfrud. The knight had killed his father and there was only one way he could honour his family name and that was to take the knight's life.

The Queen was in deep conversation with her daughter and the sisters when she heard Cedric call his men to order. She looked across the valley to see a group of goblins mounted on wolves racing towards them. Cedric gave the order and a row of bowmen released arrows which flew through the sky and into the advancing goblins. Many were hit and some fell but even though their riders had fallen the wolves continued to race in to the fight. They swept in the ranks of the guard and fierce fighting followed. The Queen knew there was little time to lose and gathered her daughter and the sisters closer to her.

"The time has come for you to play your part, Livi. Millie. I need you to watch and wait. If anyone gets too close to Livi it will be your task to protect her. Can you do this?"

"I think so," said Millie, squeezing her sister's hand.

Livi stood in front of her mother who placed her hands on her daughter's shoulders. The girl slipped into a trance and began whistling, a low, quite whistle.

The prince replaced his helmet and urged his horse forward. He was at the head of the cavalry, the finest fighting men in his mother's army. He thought of the promised reinforcements and cursed the kings of the nearby lands, calling each name and spitting on the ground.

"Men. We are charged with winning this battle. It is a fight we probably can't win but that matters little. We must give everything, even our lives. Leave nothing on this field today. Let no man have the right to claim we did not give our all."

The prince kicked his heels into his horse and the animal began to trot before its rider urged it into a gallop. The prince held his sword aloft as he rode at the head of the cavalry. They reached the first line of the wizard's army and crashed into them with frightening force. The sound of metal on shield filled the air as the cavalry cut a swathe several rows into the enemy. The battle raged as men fought each other, the prince and his forces inflicting heavy losses on their enemy. But as they did so they also lost many of their own. After a sustained skirmish, the prince ordered the retreat be sounded and he led his men back to their own ranks. At least a third of the cavalry were lost, men and horses lying dead or dying on the field of war.

The wizard looked away from the battle and to the dragon. She was sat away from the battle and appeared to be asleep. Her eyes opened and she looked to the wizard, nodding as she did so. She flew over to the wizard and landed next to him.

"What is it?" she asked, the impatience clear in her voice.

"Do you grow weary of the waiting? Perhaps I should find you some killing to do."

"That would be nice. There is no sign of the knight so I must find something else to occupy me until he shows his cowardly face."

"Do not doubt his courage. That could be your undoing."

"I fear no man, not even that knight. If you know where he is, tell me and I will tear his heart out."

"Unfortunately I don't and that concerns me as much as anything. But enough of this. I want you to fly to the far end of the valley. There you will find the Queen and the princess. I want them killed. The princess must not be allowed to finish the song she is whistling. It is their only hope and the only way we can be defeated. If she finishes that song we will be defeated. She must not be allowed to finish the song. Do you understand?"

"I do," said the dragon as she flew off.

The Queen watched as the guard fought bravely to hold off the goblins. She knew she had to be patient as the song her daughter was whistling was an ancient one and the task could not be rushed. The sisters were standing patiently next to her and she admired their courage. If she had been asked to do the same when she was their age she knew she would have been petrified.

One sound made her heart sink. It was the sound of a dragon screeching at the top of its voice. A dark shadow covered the mound where they stood as the dragon flew overhead. It arced back towards them and swooped down with talons outstretched ready to crash into their small group.

"Now, Millie, now," cried the Queen.

The young girl moved swiftly and a bright light encircled them. The light was so bright the goblins were immediately forced back and had to cover their eyes. Even the dragon was blinded and crashed into some nearby trees. As it recovered its senses the dragon could do nothing about the searing pain which the light caused every time it looked in its direction. The dragon launched itself off the ground and flew away quickly, seeking safety anywhere away from the light.

The wizard could see the light and cursed loudly. The witch tried to comfort him but he cast her aside and she fell to the ground. She turned her face to his and began to cry, beating the ground with her clenched fists and cursing like a chastised child. The wizard knew he was running out of ideas but could think of nothing. He was worried now that a battle it seemed impossible to lose was being lost, a certain victory was slipping from his grasp. It was time to leave but he would not go without making his mark.

The wizard raised both of his hands high above his head and a bright light arced between his fingers. A bolt of fire shot from his hands and flew into the massed ranks of the Queen's soldiers, quickly followed by half a dozen more. Where the soldiers had stood all that remained was scorched and blackened earth. The wizard smiled to himself before turning and walking from the battlefield.

The Queen looked on in horror and felt helpless. She willed her daughter to finish so that the battle and its needless slaughter could be ended.

The dragon watched the wizard leave but that did not concern her. She was scanning the lines of the Queen's men, looking for the knight. She was startled from her searching by the sound of a horn. From the trees along one side of the valley emerged a vast army of men mounted on horses. At their head was a man clad in shining armour. It was Yksboor. The knight had returned. A smile came to the dragon's face and a warmth filled her heart. At last the time to avenge her daughter's death had arrived.

Yksboor searched the sky until he found the dark shape he knew would be there. He kicked his horse and rode down in to the valley where he came face to face with the dragon as it swooped down to meet him. The knight lifted his spear in his right arm and threw it at the advancing dragon. The beast was taken by surprise as the weapon arced towards it. The dragon reached out with its left foreleg and tried to beat the spear away. The dragon only managed to keep the spear away from its head and was alarmed to see it embed itself in her left shoulder. She cried out in pain and gripped the weapon, pulling it out of her shoulder as she landed on the ground.

Yksboor was heartened by the injury to his foe but quickly drew his sword and charged. The dragon was waiting for him and latched its front foot around the horse's head. The frightened animal reared back in shock, unseating its rider. The knight scrambled to his feet and held up his shield just in time to deflect the blow from the dragon's clawed foot. Blows rained down on the knight but he managed to deflect them using his sword and shield. The knight was knocked over again but managed to get into a kneeling position, holding the shield in front of him to block a draught of fire which issued from the dragon's mouth and enveloped him. Yksboor had not given up hope of beating the dragon but was worried he would not have the strength to outlast the beast. He searched his memory for the way to beat the beast and something suddenly came to him. It was a memory long buried of something his father had told him. The way to defeat a stronger enemy was to trick it into thinking you had lost the fight before striking the fatal blow.

Yksboor went on the offensive. He leapt to his feet and thrust the shield towards the dragon, bringing the sword to his side and directing a fierce blow at the beast's head. The dragon swerved out of the way of the blow and lurched at the knight. Yksboor was caught in the chest by the dragon's head and fell backwards, the sword and shield falling from his hands as he fell onto his back. Yksboor lay there motionless and the dragon leapt on him, pinning him by the shoulders to the ground. The dragon sniffed at the knight and prepared to bite into his flesh, drawing back its lips and baring two rows of razor sharp teeth. A smile covered its face.

"For my daughter," said the dragon.

"For my father," said the knight.

The dragon's face turned into a puzzled look as it did not understand and it was taken by surprise by what happened next.

The knight had a dagger is his right hand and swiftly struck the dragon in the side of the head with it. The blow was perfectly aimed as the blade slid between two flaps of scales which covered the dragon's skull and entered into soft tissue. The blade cut into the dragon's brain and the beast was killed instantly. The knight felt the dragon's hold on him relax and struggled free before the beast's dead body fell on him. He rolled away and got to his feet, looking at the lifeless body. A loud roar caused him to look at the side of the valley where he saw the men he had led there had raised their weapons and started chanting his name. He raised his sword in reply and brought it down with one swift gesture. The men responded by charging at the enemy ranks. The wizard's forces, having seen their leader flee the field and also witnessing the slaying of the dragon, were not about to give up without a fight. They still outnumbered the Queen's army by at least two to one.

Yksboor was about to join his men when he noticed the wizard's men had dropped their weapons. He noticed a familiar sound. The sound of whistling. He looked to the other end of the valley where he saw the Queen and the princess and he realised what was happening. Old tales from his father had told of this and it brought a smile to his face, a long buried memory of a folklore which had proved to be true and had saved the day.

The knight rejoined his men and led them to their enemies where, instead of the ghastly business of death they were soon engaged in taking prisoners and impounding weapons. The knight set his men to building camps where they kept their prisoners safely under guard in quickly erected stockades.

Chapter 47

The Queen sat on her throne, flanked either side by her children. The palace was thronging with courtiers and the happy sound of the laughter of children.

The Queen looked at the knight who was knelt before her, his sword held flat on both hands as a sign of his oath to protect.

"Arise, knight. What will you do now?"

"I only serve," he replied.

"I would like for you to stay but your oath is fulfilled. I free you to do as you please. You can remain, which I would prefer, or you can go to seek your fortune elsewhere."

"If it pleases you, my Queen, I will I choose to leave. I seek the remaining members of my family. I have neglected them too long."

"Do you know here they are? How will you find them?"

"I have a guide," replied the knight, looking to a window where Charlie perched. The bird flew down and landed on his shoulder as the knight rose and turned to leave.

"We wish you well," said the Queen as he passed through the heavy oak doors. He mounted his horse and rode through the castle gates before disappearing into the distance.

Chapter 48

The old man in the grey cloak paused to look at the tree on the other side of the clearing. A small man, small enough to be a child, was pinned to a tree by a lance. From the head of the lance a standard ruffled on the breeze. The standard bore the royal crest. The man got off his horse and walked across to the small man who heard the approaching footfalls and started to kick his legs as he tried to struggle free.

Smy was visibly shaking. The prince had surely returned as he had said he would. The prince's words were still ringing in his ears. After pinning him to the tree he had promised to return after two days. Either to free him to a life of imprisonment or to bury his body.

The man reached up and removed the lance. Smy fell to the floor. Without looking up he raised his hands in a pleading manner and begged for his life.

"Come, Smy. It is time to leave this place."

Smy recognised the voice and issued a long tirade of joyous thanks. He scrambled to his feet and embraced the man.

As they walked away the taller man turned and looked at the tree where Smy had been pinned and also glanced at the standard.

"So long, but not farewell," said the wizard as he put his arm on Smy's shoulder.

They both mounted the horse and rode off through the trees.